THE DREAM DRINKER

BLOOD MAGIC
BOOK TWO

JT LAWRENCE

FIRE FINCH

FIRE FINCH

Copyright © 2024 by Fire Finch Press

www.jt-lawrence.com
All rights reserved.

No part of this book may be reproduced in any form or by any electronic or mechanical means, including information storage and retrieval systems, without written permission from the author, except for the use of brief quotations in a book review.

About the Author
JT Lawrence

JT Lawrence is a USA Today bestselling author
of 30+ books, and a Kindle Unlimited All-Star. Mother to a
menagerie of chaos, voracious reader, gin fan, and urban
farmer.

*Stay up all night
with USA Today bestselling author
JT Lawrence.*

www.jt-lawrence.com

amazon.com/author/jtlawrence

tiktok.com/@stay_up_allnite

instagram.com/authorjtlawrence

facebook.com/JanitaTLawrence

x.com/stay_up_allnite

bookbub.com/authors/jt-lawrence

pinterest.com/stay_up_all_night

SPECIAL THANKS

Immense gratitude to my readers
whose loyalty, support, and generous reviews
give me the courage to face the blank page
over and over again.

I wouldn't be able to do this without you.

I hope you enjoy this new magical adventure!

- Janita (JT Lawrence)

THE DREAM DRINKER

BLOOD MAGIC BOOK 2

CHAPTER 1

GLINTING ASHES

I breathed in deeply and took another step toward the pair of marbled ivory coffins. My boots were filled with lead. There was the saccharine smell of florist-bought flowers in the air—hot-house-forced—and grass, and freshly dug soil. A rampant carpet of green rolled over the ground as far as the eye could see, and as I walked, brittle brown leaves crunched underfoot.

Ashes to glinting ashes.

So much ash in my life; so much blood. I knew attending the funeral would be difficult, but I was determined to be there for the Belore twins, Eafaris and Pepin, who stood beside the empty maws of the open graves wearing their matching masks of desolation.

Why must the earth be so hungry? Why is it so quick to swallow up the people we love?

I paused and raised my fingers to my temple, which hadn't stopped throbbing since I received the invitation to Ametrix and Francis Belore's funeral, embossed in gold ink on a handsome navy card. The envelope had been slid under my door, the lock of which was newly repaired thanks to the orc who has taken up residence outside my apartment. When I turned the handle to see who had posted it, the doorway was empty. The Khargol guard just shrugged and grunted. Some days I find the orcish way of communicating entirely frustrating, but when my skull is in a stubborn vice, like it is now, I appreciate their monosyllabic approach. Who needs more than one word in a sentence, anyway? Not me, not today.

I looked down at my boots, the eyelets in black leather pinched tightly together with a snarl of shoelaces. Black jeans, black coat. The dark fabric made the emerald background pop. I urged the feet inside the boots to move forward, forward, toward the children and their stark devastation, but they stayed bolted to the ground.

Of course I knew why my body refused to move. Any quack shrink will happily glean your silver snakeskin wallet to tell you that I didn't want to face a funeral for wizard parents, because it's the funeral I was denied when I was the twins' age. Our parents were stolen from us too soon. And it's not just their bodies and their minds that are gone, and the fading memories I have of them—so cruel is the relentless marching of time—but the lifetime loss of love I feel deep in the core of my body. Despite the darkness I was born with I could have been loved every moment, every day. I have not been. I'm alone in this world. It's an acute stab of pain that spreads out into a deep blue ache, like a hornet's sting. I looked down at my feet, and I still couldn't move.

Then there was a presence beside me, a shadow on the ground, and a warm hand on my arm which made my skin flare with goosebumps. I turned, squinted into the sunlight, and saw Darick.

Darick!

I was so happy to see him that I launched into his arms. Surprised, he laughed and returned the hug.

While he had been missing, every time I looked at the gift he sent me—a bracelet with a misshaped silver bullet charm— I felt the same mixture of excitement and dread; but the dread evaporated then because he was standing before me, alive, and I imagined his heart beating, strong and steady, beneath his elegant white shirt.

"Hello, my favorite wizard." His voice was golden syrup on hot toast.

I wanted to punch him for making me worry so much; a clean right hook to his sculpted jaw. If we hadn't been at a funeral, I probably would have.

Where had he been?

Why hadn't he contacted me?

How was it possible that he survived the attack?

I had seen how much blood he lost when the vampires attacked him, how weak his body had been.

I had so many questions, not only about those hours of torture in the volcano, but about him. I still didn't know anything about who he was, and why our paths had crossed. My mouth opened to speak, but the funeral service began.

"Come on," he said. He took my hand and we walked to the grave site together, and this time my legs obeyed my brain; no doubt fooled by Darick's voice. We joined the other wizards and witches and orcs as they stared with swollen eyes at the mounds of red African soil. I expected Darick to let go of my hand then, but he didn't.

THE PRESIDING ALCHEMIST, dressed in white robes edged with gold ribbon, began the ceremony. I caught Ferra's eye, and she winked at me. The dwarf had brought her whole family with her, including her husband Fig and their twelve children, and they surrounded the Belore twins, keeping them afloat like a raft in a green sea. Salty was there, too, but being the only goblin present she hung back, opting to stand at the fringe of the gathering. There were not many wizards who I recognized. I don't attend the annual MagicCon in Cape Town or belong to any wizarding committees. I don't have the luxury of spare time; my job as a paranormal private-eye keeps me on my toes, working 24/7 to keep food on my rickety kitchen table, and even then, sometimes that table is bare. If I had any kind of trust fund—like most of the wizards my age—then it may have been different, but as it is, I don't have the time or energy for politics; I prefer to keep to myself. Besides, I have Morgan: an untouched human cop with brass balls and a penchant for high heels and lipstick; and I have Ferra: an absurdly clever huge-hearted dwarf. They are my tribe. I don't need anyone else.

The chanting alchemist lit the incense and swung the glittering thurible above the coffins, sending sandalwood-scented smoke cascading over them, reminding me of the fog in the Obsidian Hill forest. The carnivorous cocoon, the reckless rats, the scuttling shadows were etched into my memory. I shuddered and straightened my spine, pushing the thoughts away. Darick shot me a look of concern, shivering despite the sunshine on my back. I hoped that particular haunted pocket realm had disappeared and taken its nightmarish creatures with it, but, of course, there was no way of knowing without the HighFire Crown.

THE ALCHEMIST BEGAN TALKING, and my mind wandered as I watched the oak trees surrounding us in the magical cemetery turn from green to autumn colors, and finally to brown. At the end of his address a wind whipped up and stripped the trees of the dry leaves and laid them on the ground, leaving the limbs crisp and bare against the clear sky.

The undertaker had done a commendable job on Ametrix's face. When I had found his body buried at the foot of a blank tombstone the wizard was in no state to be seen, but just the right blend of healing incantations and formaldehyde meant that they were able to have an open casket today, and Eafaris and Pepin could finally say goodbye to their father, who they hadn't seen since that day he disappeared on his way to a Council meeting. Both Francis and Ametrix were dressed in their formal wizard robes, and both held their wands to their chests. The alchemist laid the censer down on the dais, then walked over to Francis Belore's body. He placed painted pebbles over her eyelids, marked with eyes the colour of her own, so that she could see where she was going in the Afterlife. Then the twins stepped forward and put a silver coin in each of her hands, so that she could pay the Ferryman. The same ritual was repeated for Ametrix, and witnessing the brave-faced children touch their parents for the last time sent a wave of sobs and sniffles through the gathering. When Eafaris and Pepin returned to where Ferra was standing, she pulled them both close, and Fig and the dwarf children shored them up.

In front of the Belore twins stood the purple-beribboned oak saplings; their leaves fluttering in the breeze. My eyes stung and my head blazed. I blinked up at the sky, trying to clear the tears, and avoid watching the coffins being closed.

When the alchemist gave the first signal, all the wizards took out their staffs and spellsticks and held them at the ready. I let go of Darick's hand and unclipped my silver wand; I held it out toward the coffins and it trembled in my hand. On the second signal we all chanted softly together.

"Contendis. Contendis. Contendis."

Our gentle streams of magic flowed forward, all different shades and shapes, and combined at the coffins to lift them up. With my other hand I wiped the rogue tear that was making its way down my cheek. We held Ametrix and Francis Belore in our magic for two minutes of silence, then the alchemist gave us the third signal, and we lowered the coffins slowly into the ground, and put our wands away.

The alchemist began reciting his Latin verse and moved over to the twin heaps of soil, taking a handful of each, and threw one mound into each grave. The desolate sound of that first handful of soil hitting the lid of the coffin will stay with me forever, occupying the same space in my brain as along the poignant melody of the MorningLark Harp that killed Francis and almost killed me. I hear the harp playing in my mind in dark, lonely moments: watching the beginning of the sunrise; arriving home to a (mostly) empty house; tossing and turning in my cold bed. It's always there, knotted in my head.

One by one, we all took our handfuls of red soil and threw it on top on the caskets.

Two orcs in uniforms appeared with shovels, but one of the wizards in the gathering marched forward with a grim look on his face, and stopped them. He took one of the shovels, pushed up his sleeves, and began to fill in Ametrix's grave. Another wizard came forward and took the other spade from the orc, and started work on Francis's grave. The oak tree saplings were placed in the center of each hole, and more soil was added. The saplings sprouted soft new leaves, as did all the enchanted oaks that surrounded us, and soon the cemetery was green again. More wizards stepped in to shovel, and the hollows were soon filled. Despite staring at the bright new leaves of the young trees, my heart felt dark and cold, as if it had been buried deep in the soil along with the Belores.

CHAPTER 2

THE COPPER COG AND ALE

he Copper Cog and Ale bustled with waiters, and the air was rich with the aromas of Ferra's glorious cooking. The copper bar counter and the pipes all around shone and twinkled in the warm light. The needles on the vintage dials waved, and the glorious rivet-stamped steampunk clock ticked conscientiously on the wall, but no one heard it above the chatting, or paid it any attention. I sat at the main table, across from Eafaris and Pepin. Darick was at my right elbow, and Ferra's empty chair at my left. Salty had decided to not attend the wake. I downed what was left in my bottle of Fig's home-brewed ale and felt my shoulders relax. The worst was over.

The Belore twins, who had looked like monochromatic wooden puppets at the funeral service, came alive in the warmth and coziness of the pub. Their skin changed from gray to peach as the table's centerpiece—a floating fire—warmed them, and their cheeks became red apples. They had cups of Ferra's famous saffron-infused cider on the table in front of them, which they barely touched, but just as my body was relaxing, I could see theirs were, too.

Fig had disappeared into his brewery, and the dwarf children were all hard at work in the kitchen, checking roasts, turning sizzling steaks, whipping cream. When Ferra appeared with a huge platter of food, her horned helmet sitting just a little askew on her head, the people gathered in the pub clapped and cheered. The dwarf pursed her lips, not quite accepting the compliments she deserved for her food, but looking pleased, regardless. She lay the platter in front of us, and it did indeed deserve applause.

Warm plates appeared in front of us as if by magic—really it was because the dwarf serving us was shorter than the table top—and the wizards around us began to tuck in. I've been to untouched human funerals before where the refreshments at the reception were as depressing as the event which inspired them. But that isn't Ferra's style.

Roasted pork loin carved into medallions and drizzled with warm garlic and herb oil, golden potato butter rostis, apples poached in port, and spiced jellies. There were chicken legs, succulent and salty, and pecan nut oregano stuffing. Glossy bread which was still warm to the touch, baked in Ferra's fiery flagstone oven, served with honey-whipped butter. Another platter arrived with honey-mustard glazed meatballs and mash, pot pies, and cinnamon pumpkin fritters.

Before I had arrived I was sure I wouldn't be able to eat anything; wouldn't be able to get any food past the hard stone I had lodged in my throat, but the combination of Fig's beer and Ferra's cooking softened the edges of my grief, and when Darick dished up a small plate of food and put it in front of me, I found that I wanted to eat it.

The children weren't up to the rich foods of the feast. Instead they ate strawberry soup and sugared almonds. Ferra didn't urge them to eat more, but I noticed that she made sure there was always something in front of them. As the Belore twins slowly turned from black-and-white to color, I felt my dread dissipating, my skeleton warming. The worst was over, and we had survived. I turned my face to Darick, looking for new scars, but there were none. He smiled at me and took a bite of his potato. I felt the strong desire to touch him, then, to feel his weight on me.

Did he feel it, too?

"Darick," I said. "Where were you? What happened?"

He looked at me and put his copper cutlery down. "I needed time to heal," he said. "I had to be alone. I was the closest to dead I've ever been."

I understood, but I wanted more. I knew he had healing powers. Had he healed himself, as he had healed me that night in the Khargol bedroom? Or was that a Mage no-no, like a hairdresser who cuts her own hair? How did he get out of the portal, and where did he disappear to? And the question that most bothered me: who *was* he, and why had he been looking for me in the first place, before all the trouble had begun?

· · ·

THERE WAS a polite tap on my shoulder. I twisted in my chair and looked up to see a silver-haired man in a neat black suit. I could immediately sense he was not Touched.

"Ms. Knight?" he enquired. "Ms. Jacquelyn Denna Knight?"

I hesitated before answering. Call me paranoid, but after what I had been through in the previous week I was almost expecting the man to grab a knife from the table and hold it to my throat. Or slide it surreptitiously between my ribs, a quick jab to deflate a lung while no one was looking, and I'd die right there in that chair in plain view, while everyone was too busy scarfing down Ferra's pot pies to even notice there was a dying wizard at the table. I may be mistrustful, but the world is not a safe place. It may try to fool you with its blue skies, declarations of eternal love, and excellent beer, but you should never let your guard down. That's a lesson I keep learning over and over.

The man gazed at me expectantly. I saw no violence in his eyes, and his arms stayed safely at his sides. The knife I had been eyeing, ready to clutch, remained undisturbed on the table.

I cleared my throat. "Yes?"

The man seemed relieved. "Oh, Ms. Knight. I am so happy to have found you."

The twins were watching us, and I could almost feel Darick's ears prick up behind me.

"Can I help you?" I asked.

"I do hope so," he said, running his hand over his perfectly combed hair. "I do hope so. May I have a word?"

I STOOD up and shook my trench coat on, then showed the man in the neat dark suit to the private dining room, which was empty. We sat down and regarded each other under the watchful eyes of the cheerful blush-cheeked dwarf portraits framed in bronze pipes on the wall. Ten clocks clicked in unison as my hand gripped the copper knife I had snuck into my jacket pocket.

"You're not Touched," I said.

"No." He pushed the black frames of his spectacles up the bridge of his nose. "I was not fortunate enough to be born with magical blood."

"Why are you here?"

"It was my last resort."

I wasn't sure if I should have taken offense to that, or not. Just once, I'd like to be someone's First Resort. I drummed the fingers of my free hand on the table.

"Crashing a wizard funeral?" I said. "Classy."

"Please don't misconstrue my intentions," he said. "Allow me to introduce myself. My name is Willard Teller—"

"I don't know the name," I said. My knuckles began to ache with holding the knife.

"I have been under the employ of Mister Blimaex Abarim for fifty years," he said. "I am his faithful servant and butler."

Abarim. Now that did sound familiar. I narrowed my eyes at him.

"Mister Abarim is... *was...* one of the twelve pins on the Atlas."

No wonder his name stirred something in my memory. If Blimaex Abarim was on the Council then it went without saying that he was one of the most powerful wizards in the country.

"*Was?*" I said. "What happened?"

"That's why I'm here. Mister Abarim is in very serious trouble."

The butler blinked at me. I let go of the knife.

"Please, Ms. Knight," he said. I noticed his fingers were trembling. "We are in urgent need of your help."

CHAPTER 3

LONDON BUS RED

My motorbike thrummed underneath me as I gunned it toward the city center. I had agreed with the Willard Teller to meet at Abarim Manor in Westcliff, but I had to make a stop in town, first.

I parked my bike outside the old building, pulled off my smart helmet, and placed it in my top-box. The box made me think about Gizmo, and I felt a twinge in my chest as I locked the bike down with a security enchantment. Morgan was waiting on the wide steps, just outside the entrance, tapping her designer heels with her arms crossed in front of her.

"Sorry I'm late," I said.

I had left the wake early (and reluctantly). Being in Ferra's pub had been like being in a bubble of contentment. I had so enjoyed the slow hour I had spent there under Ferra's roof and in Darick's company. It was as if it had slowly unwound my rigid body, and I hadn't wanted to leave. Once the tenacious butler sought me out, however, I knew the vacation was over.

STANDING on the city morgue steps—the harsh sunshine beating down on us, the glare stabbing my eyes—was another reality altogether. I took a breath and steeled myself.

"You okay?" asked Morgan, her foot no longer tattooing the concrete step. She put a hand out and squeezed my arm, then pulled me into a hug. The truth was that I was not okay. But there had been enough tears spilt that day and we had a case to work on.

"Show me," I said.

The captain of the Scorpions led me inside, and the cool stagnant air of the interior was more disconcerting than the hot glare outside. The ceilings were discolored with patterns of damp, like scudding brown clouds in bad dreams, and the walls held years of fingerprint grime. In my mind I could hear the whispers of all the people who had passed through this stained corridor, and all the warmth my body still held from the reception at *The Copper Cog* evaporated.

Morgan banged open the double doors and we walked into the room with its refrigerated drawers. Last time the only body on display was Liz Durison's, and I remembered clearly how she looked, how she smelled, and I swallowed hard and blinked my eyes and forced myself to focus. This time there were seven gurneys topped with seven shrouded bodies.

Lucky number seven. Lucky if you're the killer, that is, not the other way around. But I was determined to reverse that fortune.

"Seven?" I said.

"Eight in total—that we know of—if you include my neighbor. Liz Durison."

Number eight: garden gate.

"I remember her name," I said. I remembered her naked body abandoned on the black lawn. I didn't see it with my own eyes but the picture was as clear in my head as if I had.

How could I forget Liz Durison? She still haunted me, still appeared to me in vulnerable moments, swilling rosé, demanding her justice. No, she wouldn't be forgotten. Not until I figured out who had done this to her and the dead women surrounding us.

MORGAN UNZIPPED the first body bag, and I saw her nose twitch. No matter how hardened you become, how used to the brutality you get, there is still a part of you, a tender core, that recoils in the face of cold violence.

"Stacey Morrow," Morgan said. "Five foot ten, auburn hair, athletic build. She was a primary school teacher. The parents I spoke to said she was the kindest teacher at the school."

I unzipped the bag a little further to look at the mark branded onto her chest and my lungs filled with the cold morgue air. There it was. A circle with a "V" breaking out of it, and two lines crossing it. The anarchy sign turned upside-down. Morgan stepped away and unzipped the next body, and the next, and the next, until all the body bags were open and we were surrounded by their waxen skin and unseeing eyes.

"Tammy Bachman," said Morgan. "Medical student. Cindy Port. Sous chef. Belinda Murray. Carey Smith. Vanessa Karkaroff. Just killed and left under the stars."

I remembered what Morgan said about the night she had found her neighbor's dead body in the garden. She said that it was like there was evil in the air, as if there was black mist swallowing everything up.

"No bite marks," she said.

This is what confounded me. I could smell vampires all over these murders, but why was there no physical evidence? And why brand the bodies? It's like someone was sending a message. This idea made me intensely uncomfortable, because as Morgan had said on the phone: all the dead women looked like me.

We looked at the last body together, and Morgan shook her head. The lipstick she wore—*London Bus Red*—seemed to be the only color in the room.

"What does it mean?"

She was talking about the symbol, staring at it as if the meaning would become clear. I saw a vein pulsing in her temple and irrationally wanted it to stop.

"I don't know yet," I said. I had seen the same emblem on the diamond brooch that Deadwing had been wearing on his cape when we were in the volcano pocket realm. I was sure it meant that he held a position of power, but in which hierarchy? Which confederacy? Acheron Baldassare's clan had no such symbol. The closest thing I found to an emblem for the teal-caped Silvano Clan—I had searched online on *Forage*—was the old family emblem, which was rather uninspiring and certainly looked nothing like this.

"I don't know yet," I said again. We looked at one another over the last dead body—Iris Beck, computer programmer —and our eyes searched each other's. We came to an understanding without saying another word. I would solve this case or die trying. It wasn't a matter of my loyalty to Morgan or my desire to do my job. I knew that if I didn't stop the people doing this, I'd be the next one zipped up into one of these bleak body bags.

CHAPTER 4

ABARIM MANOR

Biking through Westcliff as the sun set, pink and perfect, restored some warmth to my bones. The visit to the mortuary had unsettled me on a deep level. The funeral, the wake, the shabby city morgue: I had experienced such a rollercoaster day it would have given the fairground attractions at Goblin City a run for its money. They have a ride there called the ScreamCoaster—a bit macabre, given the amusement park's tragic history—and you can't visit without hearing the shrieks from the delighted goblins who live there. You'd think they'd get tired of the rides (and the junk food) but all evidence is to the contrary. Which reminded me: I needed to see Nilve SaltyS-nap. I had a business proposition for her.

I pulled into the driveway at 44 Dresden Drive and pressed the doorbell. The security camera strained in my direction and I looked into the lens. Without picking up the phone, the gate began to slide open, and I accelerated slowly along the epic driveway fenced with poplars and Iceberg roses. The dusk light on the walls of Abarim Manor dyed it orange and red, and I couldn't help feeling it was a good house, with good energy. This building wasn't based on some kind of illusion or magic spell. It was solid and old and beautiful, and I caught myself being envious of the people who lived there. An old family home, old money. Isn't that the kind of life I wanted for myself? But then I remembered that houses come with a lot of maintenance work and I couldn't even keep the cockroaches in my kitchen alive, never mind remember to prune the apple trees, so best I don't aim quite so high.

I parked in the shade of an ancient oak, which reminded me of the Belore funeral. The butler had seen fit to insinuate himself into the funeral reception at Ferra's pub so that he could talk to me, and he didn't really look the type to make a habit of crashing vigils, so I assumed his employer's problem was significant enough to warrant a visit. I locked my bike and when I turned around to face the house, there he was, hands clasped together. He looked genuinely pleased to see me, which is not a feeling I'm particularly used to.

"Thank you so much for coming," Willard said. "It's getting worse."

"What's getting worse?" I asked, but he didn't answer. I followed him inside.

· · ·

Abarim Manor was just as beautiful inside as it was out. Solid, dark wood furniture and Persian carpets, toppling piles of books everywhere, glass bell jars housing air-plants and a proliferation of exotic orchids in an antique champagne bowl. It was tidy but cozy, settled but stylish, and I felt comfortable from the moment we entered, if not a bit envious. I stopped to look at a family portrait, painted by an artist with a steady hand and a flair for flattery. A twenty-something year old Blimeax Abarim stood proudly with his aged parents, all in cocktail dress. There was a hint of some unidentifiable emotion in his eyes, and I wondered what it was; what had caused that spark of intensity.

The house was in order and beautiful, and I didn't see anything that was cause for alarm, but I was very much mistaken.

Halfway into the house I heard the howling, and I stopped and frowned at the butler. Willard gave me a sort of half-bow and apologized.

"This isn't going to be easy for you," he said.

The moans of pain rolled toward us; an old man gasping and lamenting.

I stopped in my tracks. Ice chinked down my spine.

"What's going on?" I asked. "What's wrong with him?"

It sounded like he was being tortured.

"Please," begged Willard. "Come and see him."

I didn't move. "Someone's hurting him."

"He is alone in his bed chamber," said Willard. "The only danger is his own."

A part of me knew I was crazy to continue, but the other part of me couldn't leave another human being in such pain.

Why was he at home? Why call me when it is clearly a doctor's expertise they needed?

But there was no point in asking questions. I was there and I needed to do something to help the man, even if it was to call an ambulance to take him to a hospital. I walked behind the butler to the end of the corridor, following the trail of murmurings and weeping, until we reached the wizard's room.

It was a grand old room, with arched windows and expensive-looking custom-made curtains which were drawn against the flaming sunset outside. A snow-white owl with yellow eyes watched as we entered, clawing her timber perch. The top of the vintage chest of drawers was full of old jars of medicine, cork-stopped bottles of tinctures, tubes of ointment and blister packs of pills.

Willard led me to Abarim's bedside. The old wizard yelped like a hungry dog, and it made me grimace.

My first thought was that he had gone mad.

There is a thing that happens to some unfortunate Touched people, an illness of sorts called RDS: Rasping Delusional Syndrome. Basically it's when you either do too much magic over a lifetime, or the magic you do is too deep (or dark), and your exposure to the Void becomes too much for your brain to handle, and it gets tangled up. It's like getting the magical bends, but unlike decompression sickness, there is no treatment for Rasp. When I saw Blimaex's body writhing under the cover and heard his suffering, I wished out loud that it wasn't the case. Old wizards are most at risk, even if their magic is predominantly benevolent. The fact that people are living longer nowadays means the incidences of RDS are forever increasing. The symptoms of Rasp include memory loss, change in personality, and dangerous delusions.

THE OLD MAN howled into his pillow. His fist appeared and smashed into the headboard, and I jumped.

"Mister Abarim," said the butler, but the wizard either did not hear him past his suffering, or did not care. Willard cleared his throat and tried again. "Mister Abarim!"

The owlscreeched and looked from side to side.

Blimaex lay still for a while under the heavy quilt, exhausted, and I wondered if he had fallen asleep. I was relieved, but then he startled me by throwing off the cover and exposing his afflicted body. He held his balled fists to his mouth and screamed so loudly that the sound penetrated every nerve in my body, mainlining my bloodstream with adrenaline. I wanted to run; I wanted to get out of there, but I stayed rooted to the spot, as if there was some kind of electrical current magnetizing my boots to the scuffed pinewood floor.

I dragged my eyes toward the old wizard's body, and my stomach lurched. This was not a case of the magical bends. Rasping Delusional Syndrome is a vicious, incurable, cruel disease, but this was worse.

CHAPTER 5

DEATH BY A THOUSAND CUTS

I stepped closer to Blimaex Abarim's bed, and it was like moving through molasses. My body was telling me to run, but I knew I'd never forgive myself for leaving an old man in such a terrible state. Blimaex wasn't mad. Or if he was mad, it was because he'd been driven insane by the agony he had been forced to endure. His soft sleeping shorts were damp with perspiration and blood, as were the sheets on his bed. Every shade of red and pink blossomed out from under his whole body, the skin of which looked like it had been carved with a knife, engraved from his scalp to his toes.

Death by a thousand cuts was my first thought.

The ancient Chinese execution method of *lingchi:* killing by slicing. From the Tang dynasty to the final years of the Qing, select prisoners sentenced to death would be trussed to a post in a public place, and their body slowly sliced away.

Afterwards they would be fully dismembered, so that they would be punished in the afterlife, too.

But there was no ancient Chinese executioner in Abarim's bedroom; none that I could see, anyway, and observing the fresh horror in the butler's eyes made it quite clear that he was not the torturer. I looked over at the counter of medicines.

"Is it some kind of disease?" I asked.

Some kind of new strain of virulent virus that cuts into your skin and then dissolves your organs?

The air in the room was stuffy and warm. A perfect breeding ground for an ambitious germ to grow and spread.

"Nano. Breathing mask." I said, and my nano snaked out of my top pocket and wrapped itself around my mouth and nose. I breathed uneasily through the mesh. I didn't want to offend the man, but on the other hand I was also rather fond of my organs.

"It's not a disease," said Willard. "Every relevant specialist in Johannesburg has been here for a consultation. They've tested for every virus and bacteria known to the Realm. No one has been able to help."

If he thought that would give me more confidence in solving the case, he was wrong.

"He tested negative for Winter Rage, Black Arthritis, and Serpent Flu. We even tested him for Falling Fever—which I'm sure you know is an extremely painful procedure—but we were desperate and out of options. The doctors have given up. There's nothing else to test for."

If this was supposed to be a pep talk, it wasn't going very well. If trained medical professionals, with science and labs on their side, had not been able to find the cause, then what hope did I have?

Willard stripped the top sheet and replaced it with a clean one from the wardrobe. He plumped the pillows and changed the cases, too.

"What about painkillers?" I asked. The very least the doctors could have done is prescribe pain relief. If I was Blimaex's doctor I would have given him enough analgesics to fell an orc. I would have whipped an IV into his arm quicker than you can say *Troll-Strength Pethidine*, and I would have kept it going till they were able to find the cause.

"He refuses painkillers," said Willard.

I narrowed my eyes at the nervous butler. Was this going to be another case of self-destruction? Like a certain mafia boss who wouldn't listen to reason, or assassination warnings? Because then this *girl wizard* was out.

"He says that pain medication makes him drowsy," said Willard, pouring a glass of water from a crystal jug and holding it to the wizard's lips. Blimaex drank deeply and then patted his butler's hand in thanks. Even his knuckles were etched in red.

"And that is a problem... why, exactly?"

"He can't talk much, anymore," said the butler, "but in the beginning, when this first started happening, he said that being asleep was worse than being awake."

The wizard rolled onto his stomach and yelped. New incisions on his shoulders bled brightly.

"I fail to see how that could be the case," I said.

"There is something waiting for him in his dreams," said Willard, pushing his glasses up the bridge of his nose. "Every time he nods off he wakes up screaming like a child with night terrors."

I looked at Blimaex's shredded skin and thought of *Nightmare on Elm Street,* and how it fueled a generation of insomniacs. Great. So I was dealing with a magical mixture of an ancient Chinese torture method, and Freddy Kruger. After a funeral and the morgue, that pretty much made my Wednesday evening.

"WILL YOU TAKE THE JOB?" asked Willard. The owl looked at me in a really intense way.

I looked down at Blimaex again, and as I watched, a new line was carved into his mottled skin. A loopy script with hard edges. Abarim screamed and bunched up the fresh sheet in his hand, then pounded his fist against the bedside table.

I'd be crazy to take this job. Certifiable. I needed some time off after what went down last week with the Khargols, and

Pavaris, and the Silvano Clan of vampires. I needed to put my feet up and do some day-drinking and not worry about everything that was wrong in the Realm. I needed to get a good night's sleep, and go grocery shopping.

"Will you?" he asked again, his eyes sparkling with tears and hope.

"Of course," I said. Blimaex Abarim was kin. And even if he wasn't, there's no way I'd be able to rest knowing that a good man was in such unbearable pain.

Willard swept me up into an awkward hug, then stepped back, embarrassed.

"I apologize," he said, holding up his hand.

It's all right, Willard, I thought. *I also needed a hug.*

The owl fluttered his wings and danced on his perch.

"I'll get to work right away."

"THERE IS ONE OTHER MATTER," he said, and gestured to the door with a half-bow. He guided me out of the claustrophobic bedroom and into an adjacent sitting area. I directed my nano back into my pocket and fastened the belt of my trench coat.

He looked embarrassed again. "Ms. Knight. Please forgive my frankness."

"Call me Jax," I said.

"Jax," he said. "I'm afraid that there is a further complication."

Deodamnatus, man, just spit it out. I'm getting old here.

"I won't be able to remunerate you until Mr. Abarim is well again."

I pursed my lips and blinked at him.

"It's not that I don't want to. It's not meant to be some kind of incentive. It's just that Mr. Abarim is the one who pays the bills, you see. And he hasn't been up to it, recently. I've used all my savings on the doctors and the tests, and the house utility bills. And I... well, I have nothing left."

I realized then that he wouldn't have been paid a salary, either.

He looked around the room, perhaps wondering which antiques he could auction. "I will certainly find a way to pay for your excellent services, Ms. Knight," he said.

"It's okay," I said, sighing inwardly. "I understand."

So much for groceries. Sometimes I thought of my fridge as cursed. What better place to house a doomed fridge than a haunted apartment?

The Case of the Cursed Refrigerator.

My father used to read Enid Blyton stories to me when I was a child. One of the things I've always remembered is the tiffin in *The Magic Faraway Tree*. It was a cheerful little snack box that magically replenished itself, so that every time you opened it, there was a new treat inside. How I dreamed of having that tiffin when I was living on the street with the Ferals. I would fantasize about the little crustless cucumber sandwiches, the currant biscuits, the scones with strawberry jam.

My fridge seems to be the opposite of the fairytale tiffin. Every time I open the door, it's empty. And not only that, but seeing the airy yellow-lit cave makes my stomach feel emptier than it was before cranking it open, and my inner werewolf howls and scratches to get out, as if it wants to find a new body to inhabit. One that keeps a stocked larder and a non-jinxed refrigerator.

Ah, I thought, picturing Abarim rolling and wrestling in his bed. *Who needs food in their fridge?*

With a vampiric serial killer cult on my hands, and a magical version of Freddy Krueger, it's not like I had time to go grocery shopping, anyway.

CHAPTER 6

THE FERRET MANSION

When I got home I hung my trusty trench coat on the hook at the door and pulled off my boots with a groan of relief. I walked into the kitchen and poured myself a generous glass of cinnamon whisky—a gift from my favorite dwarf—and conscientiously avoided the fridge. There was nothing but regret and broken dreams inside, anyway, and I had enough of my own without adding more to the mix.

I held the glass to my chest and watched the bookshelf, waiting for Ghost to push the red hardcover off the ledge and onto the floor. I waited and waited, and then gave up, walking through a cold spot and into my bedroom. As I saw my turned-down bed, I heard the book slide off the shelf and hit the floor.

"Hello, Ghost," I said, and began to undress.

There was no sign of Gizmo, despite the miniature mansion I had built for him on the weekend. I found an old Barbie Dream House in the recycling receptacle of my building. The toy was old, sun-brittle and faded, but it had the bare bones to make an amazing home, especially for a magical albino ferret. I gave it a good scrub with detergent and bleach, then I grabbed my wand and put it to work, practicing my repair skills. It's no secret that my healing spell could do with some serious improvement, so I spent a couple of hours melding cracks, gluing broken stairs, and replacing some roof tiles with what I had handy around the apartment. I didn't stop there, though. It was so cathartic to be playing with toys again that I decided to start making doll-sized furniture for the house. So far I've fashioned a brand new bed for Gizmo, including a sleeping bag (a repurposed sock), a miniature couch (pink bath sponge cut to shape), and a table with matchstick legs, much like the rickety contraption that stands in my own kitchen. I even hung some art-for-ants on the walls. There's a cardboard welcome mat outside the front door, which simply says GIZMO'S CRIB in black marker.

Every morning since making the polecat mini-manor, I make sure the door is always open, and I top up the thimble of fresh water waiting for him in his shoebox-sized kitchen. There's also a pentacle pretzel swiped from Ferra's pub waiting for him, and in the corner, a packet of overpriced peanuts, the ones I had promised Gizmo two times over and never delivered. Hopefully he'd find his way to them soon.

. . .

It wasn't just blind optimism or delusional hope that made me build the house for Gizmo. Apart from my instinct telling me that he was alive, there was also the pot plant on my kitchen windowsill. Before I ever laid eyes on the HighFire Crown, the plant was sad and limp-looking. I gave it water and talked to it, and made sure I moved it toward the sunlight on colder days, but it ignored my care and sulked so hard that it almost killed itself. Once I had possession of Pavaris's crown, however, it made a miraculous recovery. Not only did all my crap charity-store-bought furniture start sprucing up, but the plant came back to life, too. When I had to let the Crown go in order to escape the shimmering pocket realm and make it back to real life in one piece, my furniture went back to being flea-bitten but the plant kept thriving. It grew and flowered and grew some more, and now it was taking up half the kitchen window with its fresh green leaves and greedy tendrils.

The plant fills me with dread and hope in equal measure. Dread, because if it is still siphoning magic from the Crown, it means that even though the pocket realm popped out of existence, its contents ended up *somewhere*. Somewhere close enough to persuade the plant to grow so rampantly, thus close enough for Acheron to lay his hands on it. If the leader of the Silvano Clan gets hold of the HighFire Crown, well, let's just say that the pot plant won't be the only thing considering a swift suicide. There's no way I would agree to live in a Realm ruled by vampires, especially under a leader as evil as Acheron Baldassare. But that's theoretical, anyway, because if the Silvanos came into power, I'd be one of the first targets on their hit list. These troubling thoughts speed through my head every morning when I see the plant climbing up the burglar bars, and I feel a deep sense of foreboding, but at the same time there is a small part of me that is lit by hope, because if the Crown is still around and in good nick, then Gizmo is probably also still alive.

So I do my best to ignore the riotous plant and instead work quietly on the ferret mansion. I add extra roof tiles, and carpets, and I fantasize about buying tiny little cups and saucers so that Gizmo won't have to drink out of a thimble, and I pray to the Void that he'll come home.

MY HEADACHE, which had retreated while I was distracted by my new case, returned with a vengeance, and the throbbing threatened to blind me when I walked to my bathroom, in search of paracetamol in the bathroom cabinet. The naked lightbulb seemed to be glowing brighter, as if there was a surge of current in the building, and I wondered if it might explode and shower me with its eggshell-thin glass. I looked into the mirror on the cabinet, which was attached to the cracked-tile wall, and a rusted version of my face stared back at me. I looked as pale as I felt. The tattoo on my neck of a vampire bite stood in sharp contrast to the milkiness of my skin. I stepped closer, and looked into my eyes, searched them, as if they had some kind of clue. I stared at myself, my breath fogging up the glass, as I listened to the electricity hum in the bulb above me.

Then I realized the clue wasn't in my reflection, but just beyond it. The clue was in the bathroom cabinet.

I OPENED the door and found what I was looking for. Headache tablets, yes, but more than that: the ring-shaped stain of where the glimmering purple glamour potion had stood for years before I used it to infiltrate the SubRealm beer hall last week. Maybe not a clue, nothing as solid as a clue, but the beginning of a way forward. The potion needed replacing, and for that I would have to visit the most well-respected magical apothecary in Jozi.

There were other places to buy potions, but I wasn't looking for a backstreet medicine man. I wanted the real deal, the legend, the place that even the most cynical witches and wizards frequented. It was situated in a dodgy part of town, but that kind of added to its street cred. *Mason & Sons* have been around since the gold digger days and have seen all manner of stores leap up around them, but there they remain after it all turned to dust and the new wave of commerce flew up. To say that they sold every elixir and magical tincture known to man is no exaggeration, and their philter and magical malady knowledge is legendary. If anyone could help me understand what was happening to Blimaex Abarim, it was the wise proprietors of *Mason & Sons.*

Feeling relieved, I put two bitter chalky pills on my tongue and chased them with the last of the whisky, then fell asleep face-down, diagonally across the duvet, without bothering with the neatly folded pajamas on the foot of my bed.

CHAPTER 7

PINK DAGGER

The sunrise, though pretty, slid like a pink dagger into my eyes, immediately re-igniting my headache and forcing me out of bed. More pills and a gulp of water right from the tap, and I felt vaguely human again. It was too early to be awake, too early to visit the apothecary, and I cursed the curtains in my bedroom for being so damn threadbare and robbing me of what could have been a good night's sleep, instead of a few hours in which I may or may not have been drooling on my ghost-plumped pillow.

I yawned without bothering to cover my mouth—living alone for so long has very few perks, but that is one of them —and forced myself into the shower, which, despite being owned by an orc, seemed to be designed to fit a goblin on a skinny day. The water was warm, though, and welcome, and by the time I stepped out onto the balding bathmat the drugs had kicked in and I was feeling like a new wizard.

The kitchen was still dark when I filled up the kettle and switched it on. It was still early enough to squeeze in a quick lesson for Bron, so I texted him, and he was at the front door before the water boiled. I guess that's the advantage of having an apprentice who is a raven shifter.

The Khargol guard looked more than a little grumpy when we left. If you can imagine a buff dill pickle frowning, that's what he looked like. I invited him to go inside and make himself a cup of tea but he just grunted at me. That's orc gratitude for you, but I could hardly be put out. He, and his shift partner, Gnor (who I nicknamed *Snore* because of his innate talent to sleep at any time, in any position) had been guarding my place since Don Vito "Or'Capone" Khargol had been murdered in his sleep by his wife. I kept expecting them to say their job was done, now that The Godfather was in the ground, but their boss—named, aptly, "Boss"—had instructed them to protect me till further notice, because that is what Vito wanted before he died. I didn't know how long the personal bodyguard bonus would last, but it definitely made me feel safer when I was alone in the apartment at night. Also, potential threats aside: my vile landlord, Uragh, who smells suspiciously like three-day-old orc vomit, with anchovies, had been keeping his distance, which was a boon not to be underestimated.

BRON SKIPPED AHEAD OF ME, excited for the lesson. I told him not to get his hopes up. He was still so damn cheerful before a training session; it got on my nerves. His skip slowed to a walk, and then I felt bad. Just because I was old and jaded—okay, young and jaded, but sometimes I felt ancient, like one of those illustrations of hermit mountain wizards wearing star-patterned robes—didn't mean I should take it out on the hapless street urchin.

We ran the five blocks from my apartment to the park and arrived huffing and puffing, the city smog trailing out of our lungs. In the first lesson Bron complained about the exercise, but I told him that keeping his body in peak condition and ready for battle was just as important as knowing all the spells in the book. When you have a legion of demons after you, best you have calves of steel and rubber knees. Best you know how to parkour up walls like Spider Man or die trying.

Magic is not a fix for everything, my mother had told me that day in the garden when I was impatient with the slow germination of the seedlings. She was trying to teach me the value of not relying on magic alone, but it annoyed me at the time. I was five or six and wanted to use my burgeoning talent on anything and everything I could think of. It must have been exhausting for my parents. No wonder places like the Copperfield Institute exist. I imagine that looking after a child is difficult enough without having to worry if they'll burn the house down with a mispronounced fire spell, like I almost did when I was just out of nappies.

Only in emergencies, Mom and Dad told me. *Magic is not a game. It's not a toy.*

. . .

BUT TODAY we *would* be playing around a bit, because I thought that Bron was ready to have his mettle tested. He had done well in absorbing most of my scatterbrained verbal teaching, and when I tested his knowledge of Latin incantations he got full marks, so I thought he was ready for a practical test. What he didn't know was that I had a rather mean trick to play on him. All the better for teaching him, of course, and not because I would have fun doing it.

It was early enough to find a part of the suburban park that had no one else in it, and when we came to a clearing I knew it would be the perfect place. We'd have around twenty minutes before the city really woke up, and I planned to use them well. I looked up at the trees and sniffed the air. It was hardly forest quality but it did have a green tinge to it. Pollution with a dash of pine.

Johannesburg is the most treed city in the world. If you send a drone over it you can almost mistake it for a forest. That is, until you hit the city proper, which comprises skyscrapers and smokestacks, bright lights and faded billboards; or the tin roof atlas of the informal settlements: an unwelcome reminder of the vast scale of poverty in the country, the effects of urbanization, and the deep and indelible legacy of apartheid.

"OKAY, BRON," I said. "Show me what you've got."

I had been a street kid just like him, but I was given a hand up and shown how magic could save lives. I needed to teach the boy the same lessons, starting with the elementals. But we had less time.

Bron chewed his lips and shook out his knuckles. He was nervous, and that was good. That was part of the job. Being scared as hell but knowing how to sling spells, anyway.

"Control fire!" I shouted, and his eyebrows lifted. "Fire!" I shouted again.

He frowned, and focused, and lifted his hands in front of his grubby T-shirt. "*Ignem Exquiris!*" he shouted, and his palms sparked orange.

"Fire!" I shouted, and he gritted his teeth and narrowed his eyes.

"*Ignem Exquiris!*" he yelled, and a comet of yellow flames shot out of his hands, as if he were a fire breather at a hippie festival.

"Yes! Again! Fire!"

His nostrils flared and he tensed his jaw again. "*Ignem Exquiris!*" he shouted, and the fireball was so large, and so hot, that I took a step back in surprise.

"Nice work, Bron," I said, my fingers shooting up to my eyebrow to check if they were still there. My cheeks were hot to the touch.

The urchin's eyes were the size of dwarf dinner plates. He couldn't believe what he had done.

"Ready for the next one?" I asked, and he nodded.

"Control ice!" I shouted.

Again he needed some time, but then he focused and his fingers tensed: "*Glaciem Exquiris!*"

White snow fluttered from his fingers. "*Glaciem Exquiris!*" he said again, this time starting to enjoy the spell as he watched the ice flow from his hands and decorate a nearby tree with icicles. He spun to look at me, his mouth open.

"Good," I said. "Very good."

I saw some of the tension leave his body.

"Control wind!" I said.

He looked at me, lost for a second.

"Wind," I said. "*Ventum.*"

Bron clenched his fists and relaxed them, then said "*Ventum Exquiris!*" and a cool breeze hit us like a wave.

I unclipped my wand. "This is how you whip it up," I said, and used my wand to stir up the wind. "*Ventum, ventum, ventum,*" I murmured. "*Ventum Exquiris!*"

The breeze turned into a gale that swirled around us. We were in the middle of a magical whirlwind of sand, pinecone scales and green sparks. Bron looked at me, then up at the twister, and he laughed in wonder. The dust flew into our eyes and mouths. I slowed it down, then, and the vortex collapsed around us.

Bron stared at me. "That was cool."

"It was your spell," I said. "Your magic. I just incited it."

The boy smiled. He thought that was the test, and that he had passed, but he was wrong.

Evoco et excito, nunc et semper, res ac mortales.

"Bron," I said, taking a step back and holding up my wand. "Look behind you."

CHAPTER 8

THE TEST

Bron turned around and saw the werewolf standing at the edge of the small clearing. His evil amber eyes were fixed on us as he let out a low growl. He wore a mangy pelt and his black lips were wet with saliva. His ribs showed like the bars of a xylophone. He hadn't eaten in a long time. The boy jolted and took a few steps backwards, following in my footsteps.

I held out my wand in the wolf's direction, but he wasn't fazed. He started loping toward us, sniffing the air.

"What do we d-do?" stuttered Bron. I could sense that he wanted to take his raven form and fly away.

You can't always fly away, Bron.

"You've just performed three elemental spells perfectly," I whispered. "You know what to do."

His hands were trembling when he held them out this time. The animal kept advancing, but Bron was silent.

"Bron," I said. "Best start thinking of a spell or that wolf will be swallowing you whole like Little Red Riding Hood."

The growling beast came closer, still, and Bron remained silent. The sound of his snarl sent adrenaline flowing through my veins. The wolf started running in our direction, snapping its jaws, and Bron shouted in fear and lifted his arms to protect his face as the werewolf leapt up into the air toward him.

"Bron!" I shouted, but he didn't respond.

"*Rumpis!*" I shouted, using my wand as a sword, and slashing at the wolf just before he sank his yellow teeth into Bron. The creature whined as my wand smashed right through him, and he went up in a cloud of sour-smelling smoke.

Bron, knocked backwards onto the ground in shock, looked up and blinked, scared and confused.

FAIL! I wanted to shout. *FAIL, FAIL, FAIL!*

If that had been a real wolf, Bron would have been breakfast.

I helped him up.

"Sorry," he said. "I don't know what—."

"You choked," I said. "It happens."

I thought of the time at The Jupiter Drawing Room where my magic had fizzled out at exactly the wrong moment and allowed the bloodthirsty Desdemona to escape out of the window. The shame still stings my cheeks, despite having later ashed her on a grimy city pavement. I squeezed the boy's shoulder, which was shaking.

"It happens, Bron. This is the lesson. Fear augments magic. Pain augments magic. You need to use the emotions you feel. Don't let them paralyze you. Use them to your advantage."

Easier said than done, of course. I ruffled his dreadlocks.

"Feel the fear, Bron. Use it."

Evoco et excito, nunc et semper, res ac mortales.

This time I conjured the chimera of a small dragon. It perched at the top of a nearby Jacaranda tree flush with purple blossoms. I made it mean-looking and ugly, with shimmering metallic scales.

"Ready?" I asked.

Still shaking, Bron nodded.

"*Volas!*" I shouted at the dragon, and it started to flap its wings. It left the branch it had been sitting on in an awkward manner, as if its wings were stiff, but then batted them fast enough to lift well into the air. The dragon screeched and dived down toward us, and we both yelled and flung ourselves down onto the grass. It blasted the ground where we had just been standing with a squall of fiery dragon-breath before lifting its head and flying up again. Bron and I looked at each other as the black grass between us flickered and smoked.

With my eyes on the dragon, I employed my best ground-to-squat parkour jump and held my wand at the ready. It was a chimera I had conjured, but that fire breath was real.

"Feel the fear," I said to Bron, who had just scrambled to his feet. He nodded and set his jaw. He was ready.

The dragon circled in the air a couple of times and then prepared for its next attack. Squealing, it shot down toward us again, ready to shower us in flames. As the fire shot out of the metallic-scaled dragon's mouth, Bron clasped the air in front of his chest and threw it toward the beast.

"*Clipeum Galciei!*" he yelled, sending up an ice shield between us and the torrent. It was a great shield, large and sturdy, and the blast of dragon's fire didn't reach past it.

"Good!" I shouted, as the ice melted to the ground.

The dragon didn't waste any time circling this time, but came straight back for us, ready to turn us into birthday candles.

Another lane of fire came barreling toward us. Bron put out a hard palm. "*Effectus Adversum!*" he shouted, and the flames were deflected off his hand and diffused into the sky above us.

"Good," I said. He grimaced and shook his hand; the skin was scorched black. I sympathized; I knew how much that countering spell could hurt. I decided it was enough for the day.

"Finish him," I said.

Bron looked unsure. I don't know if he was too sore, or drained, or overwhelmed, but he shook his head. Maybe he didn't like killing imaginary animals. I understood that. I didn't particularly like it, either. Even destroying the evil-eyed wolf had been difficult, but I had accepted a long time ago, at Copperfield, that some lessons are harder to learn than others.

THE DRAGON SHRIEKED and hurtled in our direction, the sound of its leathery wings snapping in the air. My wand was raised, my eyes focused. It sped toward us and opened its mouth, which was a terror of sharp teeth and singed flesh. As the fire blasted us, I extended my arm and yelled as loudly as I could. I channeled my feelings of fear for the meek boy by my side up into my chest and though my wand.

"*Ignem Exquiris!*"

Fighting fire with fire. A comet of blue fire rushed out of my wand and met the dragon's breath in mid-air. The two streams of energy pushed up against one another at equal strength. I held it there, despite the current buzzing up my arm and burning my skin. The dragon, angry, doubled its efforts. I shouted and held it for as long as I could, but I was losing the feeling in my arm and I knew I wouldn't be able to hold it much longer. The streams of orange versus blue fire rushed at each other, neither willing to surrender, until my wand became white hot with it and I had to drop it.

"Argh!" I cried in pain, grasping my burnt hand. My energy was cut off and I was flung to the ground. A wave of orange flame burst around me. The dragon sensed my vulnerability and swooped in for the kill, hundreds of razors ready.

"Nano! Helmet!" I yelled, and my nano transformed into a shield around my head. It deadened the sound around me, but I could hear Bron shouting. I flattened myself against the black grass and waited to feel the chimera's fangs slice into me.

Death by a thousand cuts.

But as I lay there, waiting for what would have been the wizard version of the Dumbest Way To Die, no more fire came my way, and no massive jaw gripped me. I waited a few more moments, then stuck my head up, looking for the dragon, who was now a cloud of bitter *Rumpis* smoke, courtesy of Bron, whose face was dark with carbon dust. He smiled at me with all his teeth, and despite my arm glowing with pain, I couldn't help but laugh.

SURVIVOR'S MIRTH

O ur survivor's mirth, however, was short-lived.

As Bron helped me up off the black grass that had powder-painted my clothes a rather fetching shade of charcoal, I saw a flash of shadow behind him. I wrenched off my helmet, side-stepped him, and scooped my still-warm silver wand off the ground. I spun around, eyes wild, looking for the vampire I knew was there. I sensed a hint of black mist, and it sent a stream of ice into my veins. I was out of breath, and out of magic.

"What is it?" asked Bron.

The sun was higher now and the light was no longer pink, but I could smell the scent of copper crimson in the air. A sacred ibis croaked loudly from inside the stand of trees, making me flinch.

"No more tests, today," he said. "Please."

"No more chimeras," I promised, and he looked relieved. "But one more test."

As he frowned at me, the vampire finally showed himself, floating down behind Bron. I rushed to protect him, standing between the boy and the vampire, his elegant teal-undersided cape quivering in the breeze.

"Leave him alone," I said, sounding more confident than I felt. My arm was practically a cinder and would be no use to me in this battle. I could use my left arm, but if I damaged that, too, I'd be in all kinds of trouble. Without thinking, I reached for my crossbow, but, of course, I had dropped it in the volcano pocket realm, and my back was bare. I tried to drag my mind away from the memory of that realm, but it nagged at me. The music of the harp refused to fade, still urging me to dance toward my death.

"I don't want the boy," said the vampire. He was young, blond, with cheekbones you could carve a roast chicken with. I hated good-looking vampires even more than I hated ugly ones, because I felt that if you're going to be a foul crea-ture, it should show on the outside, too. You don't see the orc Hammerskins going for facials, do you? They don't have their eyebrows plucked. They shave their scalps on zero and pull on a stinking vest, just as orc neo-nazis should do.

Vampires should be revolting to look at, but unfortunately the Realm doesn't work that way. Mugshots of serial killers will mostly illustrate the same point, although, as Morgan has correctly pointed out in the past, there are exceptions to every rule. I hated that the vampire was lovely to look at, and I hated myself for even thinking it. I wanted him in a pile of ash, and that included his electric eyes and poultry-carving cheekbones.

"I don't have the HighFire Crown anymore," I said.

The vampire laughed. "And you expect us to believe you."

"Really," I said. "I don't. I lost it in Deadwing's pocket realm. It's probably molten lava by now."

"Convenient story," he said, his lips quirked in an unpleasant smile. Still infuriatingly good-looking.

"I don't know how to prove it to you."

"We know you have the Crown, Wizard," he said. "Let's just say we have our own proof."

"Right," I said. "And what's that?"

"We have eyes all over the Realm," he said.

Where have I heard that before? It's what Sugar Shagar told me before she poisoned her husband and ran off with his personal bodyguard.

"And tell me," I said. "What do these multitudes of eyes you have, see?"

I was getting a crick in my neck from looking up at him, and the sun was bright. I wished I could end the conversation, there and then, but my arm had completely stiffened up, and the Void energy felt very far away.

Blondie slid a phone out of his back pocket and showed me the screen. The photo was of the plant on my kitchen windowsill. The picture had been taken from inside the house.

My nerves jangled. Oh, no. Poor Gnor. I imagined his bulky frame listing over in the white plastic garden chair outside my front door, blood streaming down and staining his dark guard uniform.

"So I have a green thumb," I said, my breath catching. "Is that a crime?"

The vampire chuckled, and then his face lost its humor and he moved toward us. "You have no idea, do you?"

I didn't give him the satisfaction of an answer.

"You have no clue about what we know. We know every-thing about you."

"Sure," I said.

"You don't have to believe me, but the file we have on you is... well, let's just say it takes up a considerable amount of space."

File? What now?

"Born on the 12th of May, 1991, in Jo'burg General Hospital."

"What?"

I didn't even know that.

"Weighing 3.2kg. APGAR score of 10 out of 10."

I just stared at him. I knew I had been born in May, or had thought so, anyway. I guessed that I had been born in Jo'burg, but had never known for sure.

"Imagine that," said the vampire. "Three seconds old and you're scoring full marks on a test. I guess that's what's expected of a baby born to parents like yours."

Don't you dare speak about my parents, I wanted to say. But I was desperate to know more.

"Do you know... my name? My surname? My parents' names?"

I knew I was making myself vulnerable, but in that moment I didn't care. If I could just discover a small part of my past, a detail or two, I'm sure I'd be able to unlock everything I wanted to know.

"It's all here," he said, pointing to his phone. "Your parents, the house you grew up in, your records from the Copperfield Institute. Everything."

I looked longingly at the phone. I wanted it so badly. Just to know my parents' names.

"There may be details of a small trust fund that is due to you. The executor of the wills couldn't find you after you ran away."

"You're lying," I said, but I didn't think he was.

"There are even photos of all of you. The who-o-ole Happy Family."

To see their faces again.

"It's a trick," said Bron, breaking the spell that my yearning had over me.

"It's no trick," said the vampire. "I really will hand it over, if you decide to give me what I came for."

"I wish I could," I said, and I meant it. It was a good thing I didn't have the Crown, because who knows what I would have sacrificed to see the faces of my parents again. Of course, they were in my memory, but the pictures were obscured by age. The cruel truth was that the only clear picture I still have of their faces is of the day I found them, drained and dead.

"It seems we are at an impasse," said the vampire. "This is not how I wanted this encounter to go."

"You wanted me to smile, and hand it over."

I wasn't expecting the vague disappointment, the easy shrug of his shoulders. I had expected hissing, and his white fangs at my throat.

He smiled again. "That would have made my day easier."

"But now you're going to have to kill me," I said.

He angled his head and looked into my eyes.

Not today, he said, without talking. His eyes twinkled.

"A vampire, showing mercy?" I said. "I don't buy it."

"It's not about mercy," he said. "We need you alive, if you're going to give us what we want."

"I'll never give you what you want," I said.

"Really?" he asked, holding up his phone again. "Take some time to think it over."

"I won't change my mind," I said, not quite believing the words as they left my mouth.

To know their names, to see their faces. To visit the trees planted over their graves twenty years ago.

"I'll be back," he said. "And hopefully we can come to an arrangement."

I dusted my hands. "Don't waste your time."

He smiled again; handsome and vile. "I like you, Jacquelyn Denna Knight," he said.

My surname rang hollow when he said it. A Copperfield-appointed label for an orphan. Bishop; Pawn; Rook; Knight.

I wanted to say something combative, something that would tell him in no uncertain terms that if he ever came back to me I'd ash him without a second thought. But my mouth remained empty of words.

Bishop; Pawn; Rook; Knight.

He bowed his head, shot off into the shadows of the trees, and the black mist cleared.

CHAPTER 10

MASON & SONS

I walked the last few blocks toward the magical apothecary of *Mason & Sons*, despite it being located in a dodgy part of the city. A part of me felt self-destructive—which was ironic considering that I had spent the last couple of hours fighting to stay alive—and the other part of me felt invincible.

Just let a downtown mugger try to hurt me, I thought. Just let a hijacker jump out from under a graffitied urine-splashed bridge and try to take my bike away from me. I'd whip a *Rumpis* on him before he knew what was cracking.

My mind kept going over and over what Blondie had said. They knew everything about me. They knew more about me than I knew about myself. My parents used to call each other playful nicknames, and I grew up knowing them as Mom and Pops; Gin and Flu; Bok and Barackas. Even those names seem made up, now. Some nights, on the streets, I used to try to expunge the pictures of them I had in my head. It was just too painful for me to think of what I had lost. Other nights I'd carefully try to reconstruct the memories that faded like weathered billboards in the sun.

Did this really happen? Did that?

How much of my childhood did I make up to comfort myself on those cold nights on the street?

There was no one to ask.

I reached the entrance of *Mason & Sons*, and a dwarf porter in a maroon suit with silver piping and tassels looked me up and down. The outside of the store was large, the walls and window frames painted in black enamel paint. The name of the store was set in handsome gold lettering over the generously sized front doors. I flashed my wand at the porter, and he bowed and let me enter. A small bell tinkled above my head, and a snow-bearded wizard swooped over to help me.

THE VAST STORE was crammed to the rafters with all manner of botanicals, salves, powders and potions. Overburdened shelves reached all the way up to the ceiling, every available space taken by some or other magical ingredient. I could smell the incenses and the oils as they all blended together to create a heady perfume of potential enchantment. In the center of the store, over the main counter, hung a giant stuffed crocodile, its taxidermal jaws turned artfully into a mean and subtle grin.

"How can I help you today, Miss?" the grizzled wizard said. I guessed he was two hundred years old in the shade, and had the skin to prove it. In a totally inappropriate flash-daydream I imagined him stuffed and hung alongside the predatory reptile when his time was up, forever watching the comings and goings of the famed apothecary with varnished marbles for eyes.

"I HAVE A RATHER INTERESTING CASE," I said. "Is there someone I could consult?"

The old wizard bit his lips and nodded. "Of course," he said, "of course."

He led me to a more intimate part of the shop, wallpapered with yellowed newspaper, and gestured for me to take a seat.

"My father will be right with you," he said, and I almost fell off the antique dentist chair I had just lowered myself into. I guess there's no better advertisement for magical elixirs than a purveyor who refuses to die.

WHILE I WAITED, I looked around at the timber signs hanging from the ceiling, painted with labels. In the botanical section there were signs for herbs, woods and resins. Then there was an incense aisle, and magical oils took up three. Closer to me was where the potions and powders were displayed: teas, unguents, inks, and something vaguely described as "Fruit of the Apothecary's Art".

The "Tool" section hosted stones, bones, minerals, candles, and other assorted items. I could spend all day in here, all week if I had the time. I was fascinated by the dodo skeleton lamp beside me, and the old stories on the walls. A rhythmical knocking sound reached my ears. It was coming from deep inside the store, and was getting louder. Knock; spark; shuffle. Knock; spark; shuffle. Knock; spark; shuffle. Closer. It was the sound of a wizard's staff being used as a walking stick, and it was taking forever to reach me. Maybe I'd be spending all week in here, after all.

Eventually the original wizard arrived, helping a shambling man along. Their twin white beards almost reached the floor.

"I'm afraid my father stepped out on an errand," said the first wizard. When I looked quizzically at the bent-over man beside him, he introduced us in a quavering voice. "This is my grandfather."

ONCE WE SETTLED into the cozy nook in the corner of the shop, with the ancient wizard ensconced in a reclining chair with a tartan blanket over his knees, I was more than ready to spill my case. I coughed, and the less-ancient wizard gestured for me to begin.

"I have a client," I said, "who is in a great deal of pain."

The coffin-dodger looked at me and turned his hearing aid up. "Go ahead, young lady!"

I described Abarim's terrible affliction, and how no doctors had been able to help him. Every now and then the wizard didn't catch what I said, and I had to speak louder; enunciate more clearly. I told them about the night terrors, and the way the lines were carved into Abarim's skin as I stood there watching.

"I thought it was a virus," I said. "Some kind of flesh-eating disease. But then I saw the way the incisions appeared. It was as if someone invisible was standing right there, with a scalpel."

The old fossil cleared his throat, and rested his arthritic hands on the top of his staff.

"What you describe," he said, then cleared his throat again in an unpleasant and protracted manner.

What did he have down there? I wondered. *Spiderwebs, perhaps. Old handkerchiefs? Tumbleweed?*

"What you describe," he said again, and I aged ten years waiting for him to finish the sentence. "Is very dark magic, indeed."

"Is there something I can do?" I asked. "Some kind of cure?"

The wizard laughed. Or attempted to laugh, anyway, but it turned into an awful hacking cough that made something inside me shrivel up and die.

"If only," he said, when he had recovered. "If only it were that easy to combat the Dark Arts."

My body sagged in despair. I couldn't leave Abarim to suffer, but it seemed that there was nothing I could do. I felt useless.

"And you," said the ancient one, his long white beard trembling. "You're nothing but a girl."

"Grandfather," scolded the younger wizard, giving me a nervous glance. "Girls... I mean *women*... can be wizards, too."

"So I've been told," he scoffed into his rag of a hanky. "So I've been told." He eyed me over the top of his staff. "But look at this slip of a thing."

I'm hardly a *slip of a thing*. I do one-armed push-ups and can climb a building in less than thirty seconds. I can ash a dozen vampires in the heart of a shimmering volcano, and jump over a river of lava lifting the deadweight of not one, but two children. But there's no sense in arguing with a monument to decrepitude, especially if you need his help.

"This slip of a thing," he said again, to make sure I heard it. "What could she possibly do in the face of pure evil?"

The other wizard sighed and rubbed his face. He was clearly regretting his decision to wheel the old bastard out.

"There must be some way we can help her," he said, and the ancient man harrumphed.

"What she needs won't be found on our shelves, Boggins."

The man blushed at hearing his grandfather call him what I guessed was a childhood nickname. He may have been regretting his decision, but I wasn't.

"What do you mean?" I asked. "The thing I need? So there is something I can do?"

The ancient wizard regarded me for a full minute before talking again. A full minute! As if he had a lifetime supply. He blinked his pink, watery eyes, deep in thought.

"You thought it was a virus," he said, his lips pulling into a ghost of a smile.

I nodded.

"You were right about one thing," he said (rather reluctantly). He raised his voice then, as if he were a professor in a lecture hall. "It's infectious!" he said.

My anxiety spiked. Did that mean I was going to get the same dreaded disease? I did employ my nano breathing mask as soon as I thought of it, but the sickness had plenty of time to attach itself to me before then. I felt cold, then, and perspiration ran down my sides.

The man struck the floor with his staff, and there was a small explosion of blue sparks beneath it. "Transmittable!" he said. "Communicable. Transferable."

My heart sank like a 1912 ship in the North Atlantic Ocean which may have plowed into the mother of all icebergs. I off-handedly wondered how old this wizard had been when the Titanic sank. Two hundred? Three? Then I shook my head to clear it, and concentrated on what he was saying.

"But *not* a virus," he said.

Confused, I waited for him to go on, but he didn't. He wanted me to come up with the answer. I searched the rolodex in my brain for anything that would give me an inkling. Infectious dark magic. And then the answer popped into my head, and I could have kicked myself for not having thought of it before.

"Contagious Magic," I whispered.

The fossil slammed his staff down, and a new cloud of blue sparks burst from it. "Bingo!" he yelled.

"Contagious Magic," I said again, more to myself than to the old wizards. "The law of contagion suggests that once two people or objects have been in contact a magical link persists between them."

"Yes," said the wizard. "My guess is that someone has been dabbling with a voodoo doll in the form of your client. Someone known to him, or with access to him or his possessions. Someone with a knowledge of the Dark Arts, and a chip on his shoulder."

All of a sudden I felt a grudging respect for the old man. So he smelled like mothballs and mouthwash, and wasn't totally up to speed with the cutting edge of feminism, but he had just handed me a key.

A key that might just unlock this disturbing case, and put a stop to Abarim's suffering.

I SPRANG UP, ready to thank them, when the ancient one frowned at me. "Sit down, whippersnapper," he said, then coughed for around twelve minutes and forty-six seconds. "There is something else you need to know."

I remembered what he had said earlier, that the thing I needed wouldn't be found on these shelves.

"In order to perform Contagious Magic," he wheezed, "you need *Spiritus Morbus*, which is a potent tincture of mugwort and skullcap, aged in a belladonna barrel."

"It's on the Council's list of prohibited substances," said Boggins. "There's no way you'll get hold of it."

The good thing about being a Girl Wizard, I thought, *is that people are inclined to underestimate me.*

"And of course," he added in a hurry, "we'd have to report you to the Council if we even suspected you of trying to find it."

I fluttered my eyelashes at him in what I hoped was an innocent-looking way. "I don't need to find it," I said, and he looked relieved.

All I needed to do was find out who was buying it.

CHAPTER II

A CHILD'S ENCHANTED PUZZLE

I was both thrilled and terrified by what I had learnt at the magical apothecary. Finally, I had a way forward, a way to help Blimaex escape his agony, but it would come at a cost. The stakes were high: if I was found asking around about the voodoo serum, *Spiritus Morbus*, I'd be arrested by a Council agent before I could say Black Magic. If I was found in the actual vicinity of the tincture, I'd may as well start digging my grave in that enchanted cemetery I'd visited the day before. All signs pointed to the fact that I should not go anywhere near the stuff. But as I saw it, I didn't have much of a choice.

I was wending my way through the leafy suburb of West-cliff, a couple of minutes away from Abarim Manor. I wanted to tell Willard that I had made progress, and drop off a cobalt jar of ointment I had bought at *Mason & Sons*. It obviously wouldn't cure his disorder, but Boggins had assured me it was an excellent salve for wounds. A blend of dragon's blood resin, red ochre, and bloodroot, hand-blended with rosemary moon oil, the ointment was sure to dull the pain and prevent infection, he said. He didn't have to say that twice; I was throwing my money at him. I also bought a new glamour potion, to replace the one I used last week, and a brand new invention by Boggins's grandfather. How that old fossil was still inventing potions was anyone's guess, but as I was about to leave the shop they pulled me into their secret section, reserved only for the trusted elite, and showed me all the new products they were developing.

The ancient wizard seemed to age backwards as he told me about the leaps and bounds he'd made in philter-creation. He swept his hand passionately across the bottles causing them to vibrate against each other, making me worried they would crash down onto the floor.

A POTION TO see in the dark and/or give you x-ray vision.

An elixir to ease aching bones and make you slumber deeply, with only sweet dreams.

An incense that would clear your home of insects, odors, and murderous demons.

A lip salve that would quash your appetite, to help you lose weight.

A powder to drug your dinner date that acts as a truth serum (and a subtle aphrodisiac).

. . .

ALTHOUGH THE LATTER powder tempted me, the thing that most caught my eye, and was now in the pocket of my flapping trench coat, was a small bottle of inhalant that looked like a nose-spray for people who suffered from hay fever. It was called *Nebulam*: a magic potion that could force a vapor spell.

If you wanted to transform your body, someone else's body, or an object, into vapor, you'd traditionally recite the Latin incantation: *nebulam, fumum, vaporem tu debes evadere.* But vapor spells are notoriously tricky to get right because of the significant amount of energy it takes to force a solid into a gas. Also, they're dangerous: if you don't get the spell right, there's no telling what you'll be transformed into, or if you'll ever make it back into the same form you left. For these reasons, the vapor spell is mostly left alone by wizards. But it's such a useful thing to have in your arsenal, so when Boggins told me what the inhalant did, I didn't hesitate to put it into my wicker basket. I was sure it would come in handy.

WHEN I WAS CHECKING OUT, and counting out the last few notes from my wallet, the elderly wizard rang up the goods. The till-slip paper got stuck, so he frowned through his trifocals and tried to fix the machine.

"Boggins!" he called, and Boggins limped over. "Go and ask your Great Grandad how to fix this bloody thing."

I think my face must have shown my surprise, because they glanced at me simultaneously and started hooting with laughter.

"You see her face?" said Boggins.

"Great Grandad!" said the fossil, laughing and coughing hard enough to expel a lung.

Boggins smacked his thighs. "She fell for it, good and proper."

I laughed awkwardly and paid for my things. I imagined the Masons then to be like Russian nesting dolls, except that instead of finding a smaller doll in each one, you discovered the reverse, with each wizard older than the former, over and over, *ad infinitum*, like a child's enchanted puzzle.

As I left the shop I saw old Boggins wipe the tears from his eyes, still cackling into his scrawny hand. "As if Great Grandad would know how to fix the till."

WHEN WILLARD LET me into Blimaex's bed chamber he was in even worse shape than before. He seemed skeletal, and confused.

"He stopped eating days ago," said the butler. "But he was still drinking water. Now he won't even touch that."

I moved closer to the bed, where the wizard was thrashing

around and moaning, but in slow motion compared to before.

"He's dying," said Willard, and his voice cracked.

"I won't let him die," I said. "I have something. A lead. It's going to help me find out who's doing this."

Willard clutched my arm, and I flinched. Being in the presence of such potent Contagious Magic was putting me on edge.

"Really?" he said. "Really?" His eyes were so anguished it made me want to promise more than I could deliver.

"I got a tip, today," I said. "It might lead to the person who is doing this."

That's if I could somehow work out who was buying the voodoo serum, which was pretty much close to impossible, especially if I didn't want to be nabbed by the Council.

"In the meantime," I said, handing over the salve in its small round container branded *Mason & Sons*. "It's not much. It won't break the curse, but it will dull the pain and keep infection at bay."

The butler took it gratefully and held it to his chest. "Thank you, Ms. Knight."

The name rang hollow again, just as it had that morning when the blond vampire had dangled his carrot.

"Call me Jax," I said—at least that part of my name was true —but I knew he wouldn't.

. . .

Blimaex's butler got to work, scrubbing his hands in the basin and then toweling them off. He unscrewed the lid of the salve and began to apply it to Abarim's wounds.

The wizard, who had been in a kind of exhausted stupor, became alert again and began screaming in pain. Willard stopped what he was doing.

"Is it making it worse?" he asked.

No, I shook my head. "I'm sure it wouldn't. Mr. Mason Senior-Senior recommended it himself."

But it seemed that just the touch of his servant's fingertips sent Abarim spiraling back through his vortex of agony. Willard took a step back, not sure whether he should continue.

"I'm sure it will help," I said, not sure at all. But I was certain of one thing. I had to get out of there pronto and hop onto the lead of the *Spiritus Morbus*. That was the only way we'd be able to stop the affliction, once and for all. I just didn't know how.

As we both stood there, arms limp at our sides in despair, something occurred to me. I angled my head and tried to make out what shape the incisions were. Then I slanted my head the other way, and something clicked.

"Willard," I said.

He looked up at me, defeat pulling at his lips.

"Look at that." I pointed to a section of cuts on Blimaex's skin. "Do you see that?"

Willard frowned at me, then looked in the direction I was pointing. He was probably thinking: *Of course I see the lacerations, it's all I can see. It's all I've seen for days.*

The owl flapped his wings, which made me jump. I had forgotten she was there.

"The incisions," I said. "They're not just random patterns."

We both looked more closely, and Willard drew in a breath. "Words," he said.

"Sentences," I said. Someone was trying to send a message.

CHAPTER 12

THE DREAM DRINKER

"What does it say?" asked the butler.

It was difficult to read. I loped across the room and opened the curtain, just a little. Blimaex groaned. I recognized some of the words.

"It's Latin," I said. "Something about two rabbits. A white rabbit and a black rabbit. Ring any bells?"

Willard shook his head.

But it sparked something in my memory. An old story. A wizard fairytale. Had my Dad read it to me, along with the stories of magic trees and tiffin boxes?

The rabbits were siblings. Brothers. And the white one was good, the other one bad. It would have been banned in this day and age for its racist overtones, but the original was not based on skin color. It was about white magic versus black magic. Benevolent sorcery versus the Dark Arts.

This is something, I thought. This is important.

I felt blood rush to my cheeks. My fingers tingled.

This is a bright neon flashing sign pointing in the direction of the torturer, and we're so close I can smell it.

"Does Blimaex have any fairytales?" I asked. "Any children's books?"

Willard looked slightly alarmed at the fever in my face but he strode out of the room and I followed him, down the passage and into the beautiful double-volume library where the sun streamed in onto its warm wooden floorboards. Willard put a finger to his lips while he searched for the correct section, then after a moment of squinting at the spines of the books he said "Ah ha!"

He pulled out a pile of books from the bottom row in the right-hand corner, and blew the dust off the covers. He placed them with a bang on the small desk beside us, and I started going through them. There were the regular ones, written, presumably, by Untouched humans: *Snow White and the Seven Dwarfs*—which Ferra always had a good laugh at—*Sleeping Beauty*; *Cinderella*. But then came the books written especially for wizard children: *The Alchemist Girl*; *Don't Drink the Potion!*; *Salamander Sorcery and Other Secret Spells*.

Near the bottom of the pile I found what I was looking for. A large hardcover, scuffed and worn, the first couple of pages slightly tea-stained. A beautiful illustration of a white and a black rabbit on the cover, huddled together as if sleeping, creating the form of the Yin/Yang symbol, which was a popular tattoo in the 90s if you were susceptible to peer pressure and/or marijuana. The background was a nebulous green and blue fog with veins embossed over it. The title was also embossed in gold.

THE DREAM DRINKER.

I LEAFED through the first few pages. This version was translated into English, but it was the same story. Two rabbits, one naughty, one nice, had always wanted someone to love them. They squabbled a great deal, but then they had to overcome their differences in order to save a (girl!) wizard from a tower, who was being held there by a powerful older wizard so that he could drink her dreams, and in that way, steal her magical power. Because of this, his magic grew potent, almost to the point where he was indestructible, but the rabbits worked together to trick him and free the young girl, and she adopted them and cared for them for the rest of their lives, and, you guessed it, they lived happily ever after.

But what did this story have to do with Blimaex?

I passed the book to Willard, who grew pale as he read it.

"It's Slyden." His voice was as tense as a violin string.

"I beg your pardon?"

"Slyden is doing this," he said. He wrenched me out of the library by my arm and pulled me in the direction of the family portrait I had admired the day before. There stood an emotional Blimaex with his proud parents.

"You're going to have to spell it out for me," I said.

Qwynkle, that treacherous goblin, had said I was *slow for a wizard*, and it had grated me then and it grated me now. Also, if he were alive, he would have liked my pun: a wizard saying, *spell it out for me*.

I stared at the butler. "Start talking."

"There's something in the painting," he said, eyeing the wand on my belt. I unclipped it and pointed it at the picture.

"*Monstras!*" I said, and another man slowly appeared in the frame, as if being painted on. Seemingly happy to be revealed, he stood next to Blimaex with a bitter smile on his face.

"That's Blimaex's brother, Slyden," said Willard. "The family disowned him years ago. Mister Abarim magicked Slyden out of the family portrait when he started experimenting with dark magic. We haven't seen him since."

Slyden Abarim. The ghost in the family portrait.

"The black rabbit," I said, and the butler nodded.

CHAPTER 13

THE FIRST DOMINO

The key Morgan had given me for Liz Durison's house was burning a hole in my pocket as I sat drinking a *Copper Cog Midnight Stout* in Ferra's steampunk pub for magical creatures. I was mulling over the Abarim case while feeling sufficiently guilty about the Durison file, which the Scorpions were now officially calling the V-Cult serial killer case. It was no longer only about Liz Durison; we had eight bodies on our hands, and zero leads.

I needed something, just one good find, to get me started on the trail. I needed the first domino; the rest usually take care of themselves. I drummed my fingers on the copper countertop. I wouldn't find that first domino by just sitting there. I'd have to go to Liz Durison's house.

Ferra bustled through the flapping kitchen doors, wiping her hands on her apron.

"May I have the bill?" I asked, ready to leave.

"Nonsense," said the dwarf, then she yelled over her shoulder: "Ei-*leeeen!*"

One of her daughters scuttled out, the one with the earnest face and Fig's eyes. She was carrying a plate with a generous slice of just-baked apple pie, which she held up to her mother.

Ferra took it and ruffled her hair. "Thanks, skunk," she said.

She placed the pie in front of me, along with a steaming cappuccino. I didn't need any encouragement to tuck in. That's when she punched me on the arm and crossed her arms in a way that made me think she was about to scold me for something.

"What's this about you losing that crossbow I lovingly made for you?"

I froze, fork halfway to my mouth, and looked at her over the steaming coffee. "I'm so sorry," I said. "I loved that crossbow like a first-born child. I wasn't being careless with it, I swear. It was—"

Ferra started chuckling. "It's no bother, Jinx, no bother."

It is for me, I thought.

"Ei-*leeeen!*" the dwarf yelled, but she needn't have, because Eileen was already standing right next to her with my shiny new crossbow.

I stared at it. "Really?"

"Really," said little Eileen, who I had never heard talk before.

"Easy now," said Ferra, as the child handed it over. It felt wonderful in my hands, just zinging with potential. It felt exactly like the previous one, except this one wasn't lost in lava.

"I had the blueprint from last time, didn't I?" Ferra said. "So it was just a matter of printing out a new one."

"Oh, Ferra," I said, admiring the sleek flightpath and the elegant under-quiver. "Thank you!"

"You're welcome." The dwarf whacked me on my back, and I inadvertently pulled the trigger. Luckily the safety switch was on, or I would have put an arrow in the vellum airship that forever bobbed around on the ceiling, bumping into beams and clocks.

She chuckled at my startled face. "Try to keep this one alive for more than a day."

ARMED with my new crossbow and an intense desire to find the first domino in the V-Cult case, I decided to visit Liz Durison's house. I had less than an hour before my meeting with Nilve SaltySnap—to try and wheedle Council-prohibited substance intel out of her—so I decided to make it count. Morgan had pre-cleared my entrance to the security complex, so they waved me through when I showed them my ID card. No fingerprint scan, no request for my unabridged birth certificate, my 3D-mapped DNA profile, or a goat sacrifice at full moon. I smiled as I accelerated, wound my way around the pretty Mexican-Daisy-lined streets, and parked in Durison's driveway.

Pieces of faded yellow police tape flapped in the breeze like flags at a neglected adventure golf course. The garden looked thirsty, and I felt sorry for it. It made me think of the previously disadvantaged pot plant on my windowsill at home, and I shuddered thinking of Blondie standing there, in my kitchen, taking its photo. Maybe that's why I'd been avoiding going back to my apartment after Bron's training session this morning. I didn't want to deal with finding a dead orc in my doorway, or the scent of vampires in my home.

THE KEY to Liz's door slid in easily, and I opened it and climbed over more police tape to get in. The interior was unsurprising: vanilla wall paint, vanilla furniture, vanilla prints on the walls. It's as if she hired the same person who decorates the interior of hospitals to do her house, too. The kitchen was more of the same, except there was an awful smell coming from the fridge, which someone had turned off, but not emptied. I glanced around her kids' bedrooms, which was sad, then started going through her bedroom, looking in her cupboards and under her bed and in her bathroom cabinet. I wasn't sure what I was hoping to find.

At the back of one of her floor-to-ceiling wardrobes I saw a rectangular outline as large as a door. That was interesting. I was pretty sure it had nothing to do with the case, but I'm a paranormal private-eye for a reason. They say curiosity killed the cat, but I don't agree; I think curiosity can keep you very much alive. (Maybe they got it wrong; maybe that's why cats have nine lives).

I pulled aside the clothes that were hanging in front of the mysterious rectangle, then pushed it, and it gave way beneath my fingers and slowly rolled out, like one of Ferra's touch-sensitive drawers. I stuck my hand in, feeling for a light switch on the inside edges, and clicked it on.

"Oh," I said out loud, when the lights flickered on and I stepped inside. This was not what I was expecting. What exactly *was* I expecting? Who knows. A Doomsday Prepper bunker, maybe. A hobby room, to escape the kids. A secret wine cellar packed to the rafters with as many bottle of rosé as Liz Durison could drink in a lifetime. But I was not expecting this. This was not vanilla.

There was a double bed in the middle of the room, and I could tell from the sheets and headboard that its primary purpose was not for sleep. No white cotton spread here, no warm pajamas or comfy pillows. This bed was a sea of navy silk sheets, and a cushioned headboard: black leather, with studs, to which a pair of handcuffs were attached. All around the room, the walls were decorated with toys and tools: latex gimp suits, ten-inch steel heels, whips, gloves, ropes, and various shapes and sizes of... well, I'll leave that to your imagination. I don't think of myself as a prude, but just glancing at some of the apparatus on the walls made me nervous. I walked over to the dressing table: black; stylish, and I slid open the top drawer. Inside, along with a staggering selection of gels, condoms, and rings, was a little black book. I picked it up and flipped through it. There were columns and columns of nicknames, written neatly in black ink. I was impressed by the sheer volume of Durison's lovers. There were a few repeats, but it seemed that mostly she liked them fresh.

So Liz Durison was "happily divorced" (as Morgan described people in her situation) but she hadn't settled for a life of celibacy. She had two kids, so that must have made meeting people and dating difficult. Where was she meeting these men?

I reached for my phone and photographed the last few pages of the little black book, April to September, and sent the pictures to Morgan. I slid the book into my coat. I had a feeling it held an important clue. It may even be my domino. I felt buoyed as I locked up and left, jumping on my motorbike.

Was the killer's name in my pocket?

CHAPTER 14

OLDE WORLDE RAILWAYS

"Jacqueline Denna Knight?" the voice crackled down the line.

"Speaking," I said.

"Thank goodness," the stranger said, and I heard a rustling in the background, then a sharp whistle, and hissing.

"It's a bad line," I said. "Can you speak up?"

"Ms. Knight. I'm Tambo Vuleka, the owner of the *Olde Worlde Railways*."

I knew the company, and I knew why the man was phoning me before he began to elaborate.

Olde Worlde Railways ran a tourist trap operation from Jo'burg to the Magaliesberg, a steam train locomotive with all the fancy trimmings. You get on at the Johannesburg station, enjoy a leisurely trip to the berg, disembark for a picturesque picnic lunch at the old collapsed tunnel in the rocky mountain, then mosey back to the city.

According to their brochures, when you arrive at their quaint rail station you feel like you're going back to a simpler time of ruffle skirts and cherry tobacco pipes. Their beautifully restored carriages and clouds of white steam purportedly send one tumbling back through time. Personally, I didn't know why anyone would want to take a step back. I loved my high-tech protective coat and my intuitive magical crossbow with built-in heat-seeker, never mind the nano that I kept within whispering distance in my top pocket.

I knew why the man was phoning, because any time I hear about old-world this or Victorian-era that, or any kind of wistful setting of bygone days, I don't think of it as charming or nostalgic. I think of one thing: vampires.

Vampires have this hankering for the past like no other species I know. They take "conservatism" to a brand new high. If they had the choice, we'd all be living in grim ante-diluvian castles with no running water, and no wifi.

So these tourist destinations and day-trip diversions all had one thing in common: they were vamp magnets. Which was great for me if I was in the mood to hunt some bloodsuckers, but bad news for starry-eyed foreigners who had no idea how reckless South African vampires could be.

"What can I do for you?" I shouted into the phone, via blue-tooth, which was a bit awkward, because I was on my motorbike and had just stopped at a red right. The woman next to me, in a shiny Honda, gave me a suspicious look.

I didn't have time to make small talk.

"You have a vampire problem," I shouted, and the woman in the car almost dropped her takeaway coffee onto her lap in her hurry to wind up her windows. My smart helmet fizzed with static.

"Yes," came Vuleka's reply. "Please come as soon as you can."

I had Liz Durison's little black book I needed to comb through for leads, plus I was already late for my appointment with Nilve SaltySnap at Goblin City. I was going to consult my favorite slimeball on where to find the seller of voodoo serum, and hopefully that would guide me to Blimaex's torturer.

"I'll help you," I said, and the man swore in relief. "But I have a couple of important things to do, first."

"I've shut down the whole station," Vuleka said. "I've closed it up. But people are still coming through the gate. I can't stop them. We haven't had an attack…"

"Yet," I said.

"Innocent people are going to die if you don't get here soon."

Even if hapless strangers speaking in German accents weren't in danger I'd still gun it there as fast as I could, because everyone who knows me knows that my mission in life is to kill vampires. I'd ash every vampire in the country if I could.

"I'll be there as soon as I can," I said, and I meant it.

CHAPTER 15

IN PLAY

I was twenty minutes late for my meeting with Nilve SaltySnap, but she didn't seem bothered. I guess when you live in a goblin amusement park you give up waiting as a state of mind. I gave her the bubblegum-flavored soft-serve ice cream I bought her at The Snack Shack, and she snatched it and started licking at the dripping blue treat without saying *hello* or *thank you,* which is pretty much exactly what I had expected. Then Salty yelled "Ah!" and clutched her forehead. The ice cream was no longer in her hand. She'd swallowed the thing whole.

"Ah!" she said again. "You're trying to kill me!"

"I don't think anyone has ever died of brain freeze before," I said. I looked at her new uniform. "You're not working at the Popcorn Barn anymore?"

"I've been rotated." She pointed at the badge on her chest. It was the ScreamCoaster logo. "It's my job to make sure that the passengers are tall enough to ride."

"That can't be easy," I said, and she smiled at me, showing me all her needle teeth, which had a slight blue tinge from the ice cream. It was an improvement.

Goblins walked past us, shoveling chips into their mouths and chomping hotdogs dripping with bright tomato sauce.

"Somewhere we can talk?" I asked.

Salty nodded, and we walked to the children's area. The old cars-on-a-track Jungle Safari Ride was empty, so we jumped into an antique jeep and clicked our safety belts on. Nilve couldn't reach the pedal, so I did the honors, and the vehicle lurched forward and began its loop around the circuit.

"You said something about a business proposition," said Salty, not taking her eyes off the steel track in front of us, as if I was such a bad driver that I could even crash a car with no steering column.

"Something more urgent has come up," I said, ducking to avoid a plastic palm leaf. "We'll get to my idea later."

We passed real rocks and fake trees, and zoomed underneath a bridge and into a puddle. Dirty water splashed underneath us.

"You need information," said Salty.

"Yes. How did you know? Am I that predictable?" I was trying to keep things light.

"Why else would a wizard visit a goblin?" she said.

"I like to think we're not just a wizard and a goblin anymore," I said, and she frowned at me. "We're kind of friends, now, aren't we?"

Salty dragged her eyes back to the track. "Wizards and goblins can't be friends," she said.

Something was clearly bothering her. "Is something wrong?"

"It's none of your business, Wizard," she said, and turned her face away from me, looking out of the non-existent car window. A robotic cobra rose up from its coil and hissed at us, its red eyes glowing. A gorilla roared over the speaker above us.

I shrugged. After what we had been through together, I thought we were friends. Or as close to friends as wizards and goblins get, anyway. Looks like I was wrong. No great loss; I'd be just fine. As Morgan likes to say: *Don't cry for me, Argentina.*

"I need to know where I can find *Spiritus Morbus*," I said.

Nilve swung to face me with wide eyes. "Are you crazy?" Her spit landed on my lap. "You shouldn't even be saying those words out loud!" She lowered her voice to a dangerous whisper. "You know what the Council will do to you if they find out you wanted to buy that stuff?"

"I know." A dusty tiger growled at us as we glided past. I kept my voice low, too. "But it's not for me. It's for a case.

And I don't want to buy it, I just need to know who is buying it."

She crossed her slimy arms over her potbelly and expelled a short, bitter laugh. "You're crazy, Wizard."

It's not the worst thing I've been called, especially by a goblin.

Nilve screwed up her face. "You'd risk your life for a client?" she asked. "Don't you ever learn?"

She had a point. The case of the HighFire Crown had very nearly killed me, and the danger had not yet passed. I was painfully aware of the fact that I was Enemy No. 1 for a certain teal-caped vampire clan.

"It's to help another wizard," I said. "He's dying."

Salty's face softened. At least I was being loyal to my kin, she was probably thinking, instead of being just plain stupid.

The car started chugging up the small hill, and we were pressed back into our hard fiberglass seats, my crossbow sticking into my ribs. The ride would be over soon.

"Where would you get such a thing?" I prompted. "Do you know?"

"Not a clue," said the goblin.

I wasn't sure if she was telling the truth. Sometimes we play this game where she lies and then I know that the opposite of what she is saying is true. It gets confusing though, when you don't know if the game is in play or not.

"Not even a small clue?" I asked as we reached the peak and teetered at the top. Sensing our impending fall, we stopped talking and both looked down the steep cliff. The car inched forward bit by bit, heightening my apprehension, and then with a rushing of metal wheels on track the car sped down the incline. Salty gasped and grabbed my hand, and we both yelled as the car smashed into another puddle, sending mud flying, and spattering the fake leaves surrounding us.

The goblin let go of my hand and we laughed. Maybe we were some kind of friends, after all.

"Labyrinth," she said, and looked away. I was going to ask her what she meant, but I didn't want to push my luck.

I waved goodbye to Nilve at the ScreamCoaster and made my way to the Goblin City Hotel. I looked down at the card in my palm. When Salty had grabbed my hand at the top of the Jungle Safari Drive it had been an extension of friendship, of sorts. Not because of the personal contact, but because of the key she had left behind in my hand: an access card to the administration offices of the Goblin City Hotel.

CHAPTER 16
HOBNOB

I used the back entrance of the Goblin City Hotel, hoping not to make anyone too suspicious. The service alleyway behind the building was deserted, and it was easy to slip in without any goblins seeing me. The access card opened the grimy back door, and the next gate, until I was close to the center of the bottom floor, just outside the administration offices of the hotel, which were empty and all locked up. I guess there wasn't much hospitality admin to do, now that the humans no longer came to stay and the goblins had taken it over, turning it into an overcrowded hostel that smelled vaguely like stale corndogs.

I unlocked the last door, and let myself into the small open-plan office with gray carpet tiles and drywalling. There were a few shared desks, an empty water cooler, and a prehistoric-looking printer. Not only was it empty of goblins, but it looked like it had been empty for days. Perfect.

Even more perfect was the huge screen to the left of the room with Smell-It notes stuck all over the edges. It was the Goblin City mainframe, replete with scribbled passwords on scented paper. I slumped down in the office chair and swiveled around to face the machine. This day had started off pretty rough, but things were definitely starting to look up. I turned the computer on and it took around a leap year until the screen finally flickered on. While I waited, I studied the sticky notes. One of the pieces of paper said *HOBNOB*, which I knew was the online dating site for goblins. The password for that was crossed out. When the machine finally finished booting up, it asked me for the password that was conveniently written on the right hand side of the display: *SNOZZCUMBER*. I typed it, slammed *enter*, and I was in.

I had no idea what I was looking for. I stared at the bright green pixels and blinked. Then I blinked some more. Salty-Snap had given me this access card for a reason; there was something on this machine that would help me. Unless of course, she was just messing with me, which would be a totally goblin move. I tentatively opened a couple of folders and then closed them again. My suspicion was that this computer was mostly used to play charades and strip poker. That would explain the pair of heart-patterned goblin undies that hung from the ceiling fan, although you never can be sure.

There were the usual icons on the desktop, but there was also one I didn't recognize. The logo was a shiny black pebble. I clicked on it.

An internet browser opened, but it didn't look like any of the browsers I had ever used before. It was called *Onyx*. Was it a goblin-specific program? I typed something into the search bar, but it blocked me, wanting another password. I typed in all the other codes I found on the sticky notes but none of them were right, and the application warned me that I only had one more chance or it would go into an auto safety lock-down for 24 hours.

"*Filius Canis*," I said as I pushed myself away from the desk, and the chair rolled with me. I was ready to give up, but then I remembered what Salty had said to me as we parted ways. *Labyrinth.*

I typed it in, and the browser animated before me. I was falling down a pixelated tunnel (or at least, that's what it felt like). The black tab sucked me in as its center went dark and the edges opened and bloomed like a square black flower, over and over again. Finally it let go of my eyeballs and I sat back in the chair feeling like my soul had been sucked out of my body and then put back again.

It was the dark web. Not the Untouched human dark web, but the Dark Arts Dark Web, which was all kinds of terrify-ing. I didn't even want to know what flavor of things you could find in there. My mouth dried up, and I looked over at the empty water cooler longingly. Was I really going to do this? I knew the answer, and it made my root chakra twinge.

· · ·

WITH ONE HAND over my eyes and the other hovering uncertainly over the keyboard, I typed *SPIRITUS MORBUS* and clicked the magnifying glass icon.

The excessively paranoid part of me feared that the Council agent would appear immediately out of thin air (they've been known to do that), and slap a pair of enchanted hand-cuffs on my wrists. The less paranoid part of me thought that some kind of shrieking alarm was being sounded at Goblin City HQ and it would be just moments before the goblin security police arrived and locked me up for breaking in. Then there was the danger of someone seeing me through this computer, which wasn't actually paranoid at all because evil forces can use pretty much anything to find you, including windows, mirrors and goblin mainframe screens in abandoned hotel offices.

The dark web browser kept me in suspense for a moment, then only one result appeared.

SPIRITUS MORBUS, it said. *AKA Voodoo Serum. EVERSHADE NIGHT MARKET.*

"FAEX," I swore, and slumped back in my chair.

Why did life have to be so relentless? Honestly. Just once, *just once,* could the answer be the easy one? Why couldn't the search result have said I could get the voodoo serum from a nice warm safe place that I knew how to get to? That served crumpets and cream, and you could get a shoulder massage while you were waiting? No. Just my luck that the place I needed to go to was deep in the orc SubRealm, in a tunnel I had only ever heard mentioned in worried whispers, and even then, no one was really sure that it existed. EverShade was the thing of urban legends, and, spoiler alert: none of the legends ever ended happily ever after.

I took a deep breath and rubbed my face. The peril was two-fold: the danger of getting kidnapped, murdered, and/or dismembered for *muti* while you were down there, and the danger of getting caught by the Council. Your presence at the market alone was enough to get you a life-sentence in the black tower on Ember Island, or, if your luck was out, the Storm Bay Boulderkeep Work Camp off the coast of Cape Town.

Just thinking of the possible outcomes made my heart hammer against my ribs. I was used to playing with fire, but disobeying the Council was a whole new level. If confronting a dangerous goblin gang could be compared to a small fire in your backyard, perfect for grilling some chops, then defying the Council was like a raging furnace that turns into a fire-nado that accidentally incinerates your whole house and possibly your next door neighbor.

I WAS ABOUT to start convincing myself that I didn't actually need to go down there, didn't need to visit the black magic market—because surely there was a less dangerous way to find out who was buying the voodoo serum?—but then I heard a sound outside the thin walls. A goblin grunting. It took me a moment to register what was happening. When I realized there was a snorting goblin heading in my direction, about to find me poking around on his computer, I dropped to the floor and hid under the desk. The lock on the door beeped green and the goblin fell inside.

Why was he stumbling? I wondered. *Was he drunk on Goblin Gin?*

But then I saw another pair of slimy legs, and I cringed. I understood with an awkward sense of dread that this particular pair of goblins, despite their corporate clothes, weren't here to print out the Goblin City Annual Report.

The male goblin growled, and chased the female, who was laughing and blushing, looking over her shoulder at her pursuer. He had her lipstick smudged on his white collared shirt. She stopped running, turned around, and shook out her hair, like a stripper on a pole at *KandyKane* (if strippers at *KandyKane* had stringy blond hair and potbellies).

The male goblin growled some more, pulling his polkadot tie off while he watched his conquest unbutton her blouse. Now the pair of undies hanging from the fan made more sense. This was the perfect room for office dalliances.

I had two options: stay hidden under the desk, cover my ears, close my eyes, think of puppies and rainbows, and be forever scarred for life on a deep psychological level, or try to get out without them seeing me. I didn't have time to be locked up by the goblin police, so I opted for the puppies and rainbows instead.

It was a mistake.

What I hadn't figured into the equation was Mister Polkadot's sexual prowess (or KandyKane's insatiable appetite). For some reason, in my head, goblins in general went for a more *wham-bam* approach when it came to bonking, but I was wrong. I was very, very wrong. I was wrong on the open-plan office desk, I was wrong up against the water cooler, I was wrong shouting and swinging from the ceiling fan. I was wrong on so many surfaces and in so many positions that even I felt exhausted. The worst of it was that they showed no sign of stopping, so I was forced to abandon the puppies and sneak out of there.

I closed my eyes again and thought as clearly as I could: *Invisibilis Factus.*

A feeling of cold water washed over me. I checked my hands to make sure the invisibility spell had taken properly, and then started crawling out from under the desk. Once I could stand, I moved stealthily toward the exit, hoping that I wasn't leaving a trail of shimmer, which sometimes happens, or any kind of scent. A meter from the door—which was only slightly ajar, I'd really have to squeeze to get through—I inadvertently caught sight of the naked couple.

The view made me screw my eyes shut, which made me walk into a chair they had left in their wake.

I gasped in surprise, and they both stopped huffing and puffing and looked in my direction, startled. I stayed put, hardly breathing, hoping they would dismiss the sound and keep up their ultramarathon, but they kept still, and kept staring. There was no way I could open the door now, even an inch, or they'd know I was there. We were caught a strange frozen moment, the half-dressed goblins clutching at each other, staring at me; and me, invisible, holding my breath.

"There's something there," panted KandyKane.

"Some*one*," said Polkadot.

I held my breath, and tried not to shimmer the air (which is pretty much impossible to control, like telling your spleen to stop doing whatever it is that spleens do).

They didn't move. I didn't move. My lungs began to burn. Something had to give.

Aversum! I thought, hoping a distraction spell would force their gaze away.

The prehistoric printer began to growl. It was waking up after a prolonged hibernation and seemed hungry.

The goblins gasped and looked behind them, at the printer, which took a jump in their direction.

KandyKane screamed. The top flew open and the light under the glass screen flashed, and it started spitting sheets of paper at them. I hoped they wouldn't get paper cuts. That would hurt. As I slid out of the office, I heard Polkadot yell in fright, and I slammed myself up against the wall as they came rushing out, pulling their clothes on as they ran. I left the same way I came in, and let myself out of the back door. The alley was still deserted.

CHAPTER 17

BROKEN

Reluctantly, I made my way home. I didn't want to see what had become of my orc bodyguards, didn't want to stand inside my kitchen and smell the vampire that had been standing there just hours before me. But I didn't want to go to the SubRealm, either, so it was the best of two bad options. Part of it was procrastination, part of it was my survival instinct. Every time I even thought about going to the EverShade night market my body felt chilled, as if I were on the brink of a particular nasty bout of flu. I still have nightmares about the last time I was in the SubRealm and that orc had drugged my drink. It was pure luck and magic that I got out of there (mostly) unharmed. It's what could have happened that haunts my dreams.

I jogged the last six blocks to my apartment, to keep fit, and also to shake out the residual anxiety in my body after almost being caught by those Duracell goblins. Talk about nightmares... after what I'm exposed to in this job I'm surprised I get any sleep at all.

I slowed to a walk when I arrived, and greeted the neighborhood drug dealer. She lifted her chin at me, her hoodie covering most of her dark face. I looked into her eyes: one brown, one quinine, and I pushed open the door to my building. I took the Swift up to my floor, and watched as the numbers rose, the heavy feeling in my stomach getting heavier with each one. I didn't want to see what was waiting for me, but I couldn't avoid it forever.

I stepped out and edged slowly toward Gnor, who, as I had suspected, was listing lifelessly in his chair.

Oh no, I thought. *Oh no. Poor Gnor.*

That bloody blond vampire had killed him to get into my apartment. And for what? A picture of the plant on my windowsill. And a potent warning.

I moved closer, thinking that I'd need to call the head of the Khargol security team, Boss, and tell him what had happened. I reached out to touch Gnor's shoulder, looking for the blood I knew I'd find spilled on his chest. As my fingers touched his uniform he grabbed me, and I almost shot through the roof in fright. His grip was like that of a megaloctopus. I automatically jumped away but my arm stayed behind, wrenching it from its socket, and as it popped out of place I yelled in pain. He yelled, too, because he had been fast asleep and had grabbed me without thinking. Gnor didn't actually know what was happening, apart from the fact that he had a wizard screaming in his face.

We yelled at each other for a little longer, till we realized what had happened, and then stopped. I almost passed out with the fright, and jagged pain of my shoulder, and, worst of all: orc breath. Dizziness pushed me down onto the floor.

"You okay?" Gnor asked, his bushy eyebrows joining in worry, perhaps wondering if he had broken me. He had a sincere look of concern on his face, but I suspected that was more about his job security than my health.

"Not okay," I said. "Thought you were dead."

"Not dead," he said.

"I can see that."

"You broken?" he asked, looking at my shoulder.

My arm was hanging limply, my dislocated shoulder was on fire. I didn't have time for a doctor. I waited for my head to clear, then stood up, sparks shooting down my arm.

"I fix it," said Gnor, and moved toward me, hands outstretched.

"No!" I yelled. No way I was letting him put his rough-skinned baseball mitts on me.

He looked confused. "I know how to fix it."

"Absolutely not," I said. I could imagine the crunching sound my bones would make as he tried to force my arm back into the socket. He'd probably break the scapula and the clavicle, and also my wrist, just for good measure. But as the shock was fading, the pain was becoming unbearable. I needed to go to the SubRealm, and there's no way I could get there in such agony. I could feel the blood draining from my face.

"I broke you?" he asked.

I shook my head. "Not your fault."

"My job to protect you."

I looked at my front door and blinked hard, trying to bring the pain under control. I took a couple of unsteady steps; I wanted to get into the flat before I fainted.

"You have visitor," said Gnor.

I stopped and spun on my unsteady feet. "What?"

What kind of security guard was he? It looked like I'd have to call Boss, after all. I used my left hand to grab the crossbow off my back and get it in position. I'd shot vampires with my left hand before, and I could do it again.

The orc opened the door and I stalked in, ready to ash the interloper. Gnor followed.

I could smell the copper crimson scent. He was sitting there, in the dark, waiting for me.

CHAPTER 18

ILLUMINO

I snicked the safety catch off my crossbow and pointed it at the shape sitting on the couch, applying pressure to the trigger.

Illumino I thought, and my wand, still clipped to my belt, lit up the small room.

"Darick," I said, out of breath, the adrenaline pulsing through my body. My finger slid off the trigger. "What the hell are you doing here?"

If Darick was slightly nervous about almost being bolted in the heart by a wizard, he didn't show it. He stood up and moved toward me.

"Your arm," he said, and his voice immediately calmed my body down.

"He did it," I said, gesturing over my blazing shoulder at the orc, who had the grace to look ashamed and return to his post.

"What happened?" asked Darick.

I switched on the lounge light and snuffed my wand. Darick took my forearm gently in his hands. The feel of his warm skin against mine was worth the pain it caused.

"It was an accident," I said, wincing. "Why were you sitting in the dark?"

Darick ignored my question and pointed at my couch. The one that Gizmo loved to sleep on. "Lie down," he said.

My first instinct was to say *I don't have time*, but then I remembered the feeling of Darick's magical hands on me, healing me, at the Khargol house, and I did as he instructed. He kneeled next to me and put his palms on my shoulder. Immediately I felt a blue buzzing underneath my skin and the pain decreased to a manageable level. I loved the sensation of Darick's hold, and the way he looked at me with such intense concentration. When he gazed at me like that I felt like the rest of the world disappeared and it was just us. Just a wizard and a mage-slash-assassin on a moth-eaten couch from a charity shop. I let out a groan of relief as the pain faded completely. It wasn't just that the pain was gone, then, but my whole body was humming with the magic he had given me. Warmth flooded every part of me.

Darick moved his face closer to mine, and I looked at his eyes, and then his lips.

"Jax," he said, his voice adding to the glow of my insides.

"Yes?" I was ready to agree to anything. Whatever he wanted, I was in.

A shadow flew over his face. "This is going to hurt."

What? I had been so lost in daydreams of Darick that I had forgotten my shoulder was dislocated. Before I had time to answer, he grabbed my arm, pulled it at an angle, and the bone slipped back into place.

I shouted in pain as the shoulder relocated, but as soon as it was back in place there was immediate relief. Darick walked to the kitchen and I heard him open the freezer. Soon there was ice, wrapped in a tea-towel, on my shoulder.

"Your fridge is empty," he said.

"Tell me something I don't know," I said, still reeling from the relief I was feeling.

What was this small talk? What was the point when there were so many questions hanging in the air between us? Like why he thought it was okay to let himself into my apartment when I wasn't here, or how he almost always seemed to appear when I needed him?

Still, it seemed rude to interrogate him after he had just healed me. Again. Darick passed me a glass of water and the paracetamol from my bathroom cabinet.

"Something stronger would be better," he said.

"Yes."

"Anti-inflammatories," he said.

"I'll get some."

"I've done what I can to limit the damage," he said. "But my healing powers are still depleted, after—"

After you almost died in the volcano.

He passed an old T-shirt of mine to me, knotted into a triangle: a makeshift sling. He had been in my apartment, in my fridge, in the bathroom cabinet, and in my wardrobe.

"Did you find any skeletons there?" I asked.

"Where?"

"In my cupboard."

"Ha," he said, eyes twinkling. "No. I wasn't looking for skeletons. I have enough of my own."

"Ha," I said.

He looked at the knotted *The Cure* shirt. "You're going to have to wear it for the next few days."

"It's my wand arm," I said. "My crossbow arm. I can't wear a sling."

"You seemed to do just fine with your crossbow in your other arm," he said, and there was a hint of a smile on his lips. The lips that I thought were going to kiss me instead of saying *This is going to hurt.*

Yes, I thought, looking at him. *Yes. This is definitely going to hurt.*

DARICK MADE me promise that I'd get some rest. He helped me to put on my pajamas, and watched me climb into bed. I lay there, listening to him walk out the door, then I threw off the covers and stripped, and yanked on a fresh pair of jeans. It wasn't easy pulling them up with one arm, but I managed. Tying the shoelaces on my boots was impossible, so I just tucked the laces into the tops of the shoes and hoped for the best. I adjusted the makeshift sling and put my trench coat on over it. I wasn't able to clip my crossbow to my back, which made me nervous. On this mission I was going to need all the help I could get. I wasn't fighting fit, not exactly, but it would have to do.

I couldn't leave without checking the ferret mansion for Gizmo (empty) and my kitchen, for rogue vampires (also empty), though I could still smell the creature. The idea that a murderer had been standing right there on my cracked kitchen floor tiles made my blood run cold.

Had he gotten past Gnor (which, admittedly, wouldn't have been very difficult) or had he used a window? I closed every one, just in case, and as I was heading out the door, the red hardcover book jumped off the bookshelf and slammed onto the floor.

CHAPTER 19

EMBER ISLAND

If Gizmo had been with me, I would have asked him where the portal door to EverShade was, but tonight I was on my own. I wondered, as I left my apartment, if it was the last time I'd see it. My stomach growled, a mixture of hunger and dread, and I wondered what the food was like at the Council's preferred detention centers on the Ember Isles and Storm Bay.

I passed the neighborhood drug dealer again, on my way out, then after a few steps I turned back and approached her.

"Hey," I said.

She looked at me, expressionless. "Hey."

I hesitated. If I asked her how to get to EverShade and she was an undercover agent for the Council, my mission would be finished before it even began. What better place to put a spy for the Council? On a busy corner, where she could watch the comings and goings all day, and all night, and have naïve wizards asking dangerous questions.

She was still looking at me, waiting. I watched her blink. She was around the same age as me, but the street life had been tough on her. Her mismatched eyes, while beautiful, had the stare of a much older woman.

"Do you have any painkillers?" I asked.

I thought she would laugh, say something like *Go home, Wizard,* but instead she blinked again, then looked at my sling. "What kind?"

"Anything," I said, and then, remembering Darick's words: "Anti-inflammatories?"

She lowered her head so that all I could see was the top of her hood while she scratched in the leather bag she kept trussed around her hips, and then looked up at me again. She tossed a plastic bottle of pills in my direction, and they landed in my hand with a clacking sound.

"It's only half full," she said. "Enough for a day or two."

I patted my coat for my wallet, which I remembered at that instant, was empty. I'd spent the last of my cash on SaltySnap's bubblegum ice cream, and the last time I had put my bank card anywhere near an ATM it had just guffawed at me.

"How much?" I asked.

"I'll let you know," she said.

I looked at her.

What do you mean? I was about to ask.

But I knew what she meant. She'd be asking me a favor in the near future.

I shook two capsules out onto my hand. They were a poisonous green; the color of the apple Snow White was given by the queen.

"Watch out," she said. "They're strong."

I swallowed them dry, and they got stuck in my throat on the way down. She waited for me to leave.

"You need something else?"

I still hadn't decided if I should ask her about EverShade or not. It was extremely risky, but how else would I find it? I took a breath, the pills still lodged uncomfortably in my throat, and I leaned in.

"Where would you go," I said in the softest whisper I could, "if you needed to get something that is... prohibited?"

There was a flicker in her eyes.

"I mean, I know where to go," I said. "I just don't know how to get there."

"You have no business there," the drug dealer said. "Best you stay away."

"Usually I'd agree," I said. "But I have a client... an ex-Council wizard. He'll die if I don't find what I'm looking for."

Her face didn't change. "Let him die," she said.

"He's old. He's in a lot of pain. I can't let him suffer."

"You can't save everyone," she said. "If you go to the market you'll both suffer. If I were you I'd forget you ever heard the name."

Was she an agent? Was she warning me? Giving me one last chance to back out of the conversation and go back up to my apartment, get back into bed, where Darick had left me?

"So it does exist," I whispered. "EverShade."

She stared at me. "Your mind's made up, then?"

This was my last chance to avoid a lifetime sentence in a work camp.

"My mind is made up," I said.

Her eyes flickered again, then she looked away from me, up the street, and put her fingers to her lips and whistled.

Faex, I thought. *Faex, faex, faex.*

My instinct told me to run, but then a shadow was at my elbow.

"This wizard bothering you, Lou?" he said. I caught a glimpse of the gold painted on his teeth.

He wore dark skin, a peak cap, and shades, despite the sun being on the opposite side of the globe.

They were Council agents and they were going to take me in. My mind started whirring with what to do next. My right arm was out of action, but I could still knee him in the balls and then grab my wand—

"I'm going to the market. I'll be back in an hour. Watch my post," she said to the man, and he nodded. "And give me those glasses."

It took me a moment to digest what she said, and then I was so relieved I almost melted to the pavement. He handed his shades over, and she put them on. The drug dealer—*Lou*—grabbed my arm. "Let's go," she said.

MY HEART WAS STILL RACING when we left the corner. The relief I felt at having escaped being turned in, as well as the pharmaceutical effects of the painkillers made me feel oddly cheerful, and slightly high. Lou kept her grip on my left arm as we hurried down the city street, which was glistening with water from a spurting broken pipe. Cars hooted and tuk-tuks wheeled by as we made our way through throngs of pedestrians in leather jackets, smelling of cigarettes and city pollution. Some stores were still open, blaring music from cheap speakers overhead, and the fried chicken take-away place had a queue as long as a voting poll on election day.

We turned right at a discount fashion store with damaged mannequins in the window, then ran a block west, leaving the crowds behind. It was darker, now, and danger glinted in the black air around us.

"You're sure about this?" Lou asked, glancing over at me. I nodded. She had her bag open again, and was pulling something out. I wondered where we would turn next, but then there was a black cloth bag over my head and the cracking sound of duct tape being pulled from its ring. There was no one to hear my muffled scream as the drug dealer wound the tape around the fabric over my mouth.

"Easy," she said to me, and dragged me further into the dark. I tried to grab my wand, but my right arm wasn't taking calls. It was dark and almost impossible to breathe. She spun me around until I was dizzy and had lost my sense of direction, then pulled me into a narrow alleyway that smelled of urine and garbage and regret. She smashed me up against the wall, sending lightning bolts of pain from my shoulder to the rest of my body. I was still trying to shout when she smacked her palm against my taped mouth, and I panted to get air through my nose. My heart was trying to pound its way through my ribcage.

"Easy," she said again, leaning into me, pushing me harder against the dirty bricks. "Easy."

And then she mumbled something. I only caught the last bit of the portal spell.

"... *Ianua sit.*"

I was about to bite her hand when I felt the wall softening behind me. It felt like it was tilting and giving way. The places where her body touched mine felt electric, as if she held a current that was passing over to me. The feeling of the electricity got stronger and hotter, until I cried out into her palm, and with a flash of light we both fell through the wall together.

CHAPTER 20

FATES & FORTUNES

We fell through the wall, and down a tunnel of dust and sparks. I felt my body bounce off hard surfaces: sand curves and rocks. When we finally hit the ground, my injured shoulder felt like it had burst into flames. I heard a clicking sound next to my head.

"Sorry," Lou said, tearing off the duct tape and pulling the black bag off my head. "I know it's a rough journey, but it's for your own protection."

She had a flashlight, and the clicking sound had been her switching it on. She swept the beam of light all around us, illuminating the dark walls of the tunnel. This wasn't a regular SubRealm tunnel; it wasn't an old mining shaft or abandoned sewer pipe.

I rubbed my shoulder and glared at Lou. I was angry with her for handling me the way she had, angry for feeling out of control. But without her help, I would never have found the portal. She helped me up off the hard floor, and I hit my head on the ceiling.

"What is this place?" I asked, battling to speak with the panic and the pills still stuck in my throat.

"This is how we get into EverShade," Lou said.

I tried to remember how we got there, but it was a blur.

Lou lowered her sunglasses. "Don't try to remember the way," she said, her eyes voltaic. "You're never coming here again."

She started walking through the tunnel, hooded head slightly bowed, and I followed her. It felt almost like the orc SubRealm, but something was different. It felt darker. If there is such a thing as being able to smell evil in the air, this tunnel reeked of it. We walked for ten minutes, the smell getting stronger as we progressed, then Lou stopped.

"Are you sure you want to carry on?" she asked. Her meaning was clear: this was the point of no return.

You may come out alive, but you'll never be the same.

"We can go back. We can turn around. It's not too late."

"I want to carry on," I said. It wasn't exactly true. What I wanted was a drink, a warm dinner, a bath, and a good night's sleep. I wanted my shoulder to stop radiating pain. But none of that was going to happen until I found out who was buying the voodoo serum.

She looked at me, and I said: "I don't have a choice."

. . .

WE WALKED for another twenty minutes or so, the tunnel winding this way and that, until my sense of direction was so confused I could have sworn we were walking back to where we had come from. The sweeping beam of the flashlight and the monotony of the walk was mesmerizing, and my shoulder pain faded to a low buzz.

"Almost there," said Lou, when she noticed my slowing down. My nerves started crackling, waking me up.

"Anything I need to know?" I asked.

Lou was about to say something when there was a glimmer in the torch's beam; something silver on the wall. We stopped, and I saw the markings: scratches, and a brush of old blue paint. So subtle that you'd walk right past it if you didn't know what you were looking for. Lou gripped the silver thing, which turned out to be some kind of handle, and pulled it. A small door opened with a heavy *thunk*, and the sound of a busy street streamed out of the doorway. I stepped forward, ready to slip inside, but then I felt a hand pushing against my chest.

"Wait," Lou said. "You can't just go in looking like that."

I looked down at what I was wearing, and wanted to kick myself for not bringing the glamour potion that I had bought at *Mason & Sons*.

"Do you have a hat or something?" she asked.

I shook my head, feeling like a dolt, when I glanced at Lou's hood and remembered my nano.

"Nano. Hood." My nano snaked out of my top pocket and transformed into a hood that attached to my upturned collar.

"Better," she said, then took off the sunglasses and passed them to me.

I took them gratefully and put them on. I was expecting not to be able to see anything in the already dark tunnel, but as soon as they were in place, she switched them on, and there was a blaze of green. Night vision glasses. I looked at Lou, who was now a neon green ghost.

"What about you?"

"I'm not going in," she said, and before I could say anything else, she pushed me through the doorway, into the buzzing throngs of the night market. When I looked back, the door was gone, and an old wooden trolley stood in its place.

The night vision shades took a while to get used to, and I tripped along the cobbled road until I got the hang of having so little depth perception. I felt as if Lou had not just portaled me to a parallel realm but back in time. The scene was straight out of the 16th century, if you ignored the fairy lights that were strung up from the top of the timber stands.

The crowd was also disorientating, because there were so many different species and they were all busy talking and bargaining and dealing that I felt like I'd drown in the clashing sea if I didn't hang back. I had never seen so many cultures together in one place. Some of the creatures I had never seen in my life, and they sent my heart racing. A supermodel-chested man with an angry octopus head: a fireman's body but *Cthulhu* from the neck up. The cephalopod's greedy arms lashed out and squirmed as he walked past me, and it was as if I could feel his gelid flesh on mine, suckered to my skin, and I shuddered. I walked slowly, trying to hide my face but not draw attention to myself by doing it. There were goblins and orcs galore, as I suspected there would be, and most of the market stalls were run by them. The night air was thick with a soup of smells. Enchanted incense, magical candles, potion ingredients. Orc B.O. and goblin breath and werewolf mange. Above the hustle and bustle, the lights strung up above the temporary kiosks flashed and twinkled. The whole market looked like you could pack it up in a couple of minutes and run, which is, I suppose, what happens sometimes, when there's a raid.

A woman walked past me and gave me a strange look, and I turned my face away. She had long blond hair, blunt cut, like a cheap wig, and a plastic-looking face. I was sure it was a glamour. She reminded me of a real-life Barbie, which made me think of Gizmo's empty mansion. If there was ever a time I needed the magical ferret, it was now. How would I even begin to find out who was selling the serum? And even if I found the exact stand, how would I figure out who was buying the stuff? I tried to ignore the questions crowding my head and just focus on the next step. I walked past an old crone selling hexes and tinctures. When I looked at her face, wizened and without most of her teeth, she hawked in my direction and spat on the floor. The next stall was run by an ogre, who must have been twelve feet tall, and the next was an orc selling Bane Garments—poisoned clothes—in all sizes, including some orc-sized lingerie and comfy-looking pajamas, which I thought seemed especially cruel.

A man bumped into me. I automatically apologized, but he just kept walking with his head down. It took me a moment to realize what had just happened, and when I checked my pocket for my wallet, it was gone.

I should have known. A dark market like that is the perfect place to pickpocket. At first I felt robbed—which, technically, I was—but then I remembered how empty the purse was, and I thought, *Ha, the joke's on him.* Honestly I was glad to be rid of the thing. It was like my refrigerator in the way that its constant emptiness was a daily reminder of how I'm failing at life. A reminder of how empty I am.

A woman grabbed my left hand, a gypsy with a deck of tarot cards fanned out on her table.

"Hello, love," she said, her eyes like wet jewels rimmed in kohl. "Come here, come closer."

"No thanks," I said, trying to retrieve my hand from her urgent grip. She wore a knot of woolen scarves with blinking gold sequins, and her hair was a bird's nest of rich brown curls pinned in place with a sharp ivory wand. The sign above her purple velvet-curtained stall read *CHIRO-MANCER: Fates & Fortunes.*

"I'll do a reading for you," she said, her layers of colored clothes rippling as she pulled me closer, her breath tainted with cheap red wine.

"No," I said, but she didn't let go. I was stuck, knowing I couldn't cause a scene.

"Now you only need to pay if you know it's true," the dark-haired woman said, her makeup of glitter and charcoal running together on her shiny eyelids.

"I don't have time," I said. "Let go."

She pretended she didn't hear me, and turned my hand over, moving the pad of her old shiny-skinned finger over my perspiring palm. Her mouth moved in silent shapes as she narrowed her eyes in concentration and read the map of creases on my hand.

I wanted my arm back. "I don't have any money," I said, but this time she was so deep into her trance that she really didn't hear me. Just before I was about to yank it away from her, her eyes clicked wide open, and then her body was thrown backwards, as if I had slung a lightning spell at her. The table landed on its side and the tarot cards went flying in the air all around us. People turned to look, and I turned my face down, adjusting the hood to hide my face. The fortune teller cried out as if in pain, cradling her hands and looking at me with a face shocked white, then she started shouting in a foreign language I guessed to be Romani.

Was she incanting a spell? Was she cursing me?

I didn't want to hang around to find out. I started moving away, past the crowd that had gathered around us, and she yelled at me to stop. I ducked and wheeled around a corner kiosk and scuttled to the next aisle, wiping my sweating hands on my jeans.

CHAPTER 21

UNDER NO CIRCUMSTANCES ACCEPT A FAVOR FROM A WEREWOLF

It took a while for my breathing to return to normal. I made my way past more stalls and more strange creatures. A man, naked apart from a kilt, sang a drunken song as he hiccupped down the lane of booths. Only when he walked past me did I see his alligator tail, dragging on the cobbles behind him. A coven of young witches in bright lipstick screeched as they walked by. It seemed that I was approaching the more jovial side of the black magic market.

"Hemlock Daiquiri?" whispered a man in my ear.

Startled, I looked up, and saw a slender man wearing an Anonymous mask smiling at me, and extending a dangerous looking cocktail. He was standing in front of his makeshift bar, which was on wheels. Bottles of various shapes and colors lined the counters, as well as bowls of other ingredients: grilled orange slices, fresh sprigs of thyme, nutmeg sugar. Cinnamon bark smoke cascaded out of a silver can that reminded me of the tin man in the Wizard of Oz.

"No, thank you," I replied.

Did that make me Dorothy? I wondered.

The greasy cobblestone path beneath me was hardly the yellow brick road, but there were certainly plenty of charlatans and evil witches here. I wouldn't have been surprised if the flying monkeys pitched up, too.

"Of course not," he said. "No daiquiri for you. You're more of a vodka girl." The blue crushed ice transformed into a martini, and the white smoke streamed out, scenting the night air with warm spice. The man in the Anonymous mask moved the drink closer to me. "Smoked martini?"

"No."

The martini disappeared, and in its place was a lime Manhattan, glowing green. "Magical Manhattan," he said.

I walked away from the masked man and his bar on wheels. It was getting late and some of the vendors were already packing up. I needed to find the creature who was selling the voodoo serum before he or she left the black magic market.

I jumped as a snake in a cage hissed at me, and when I looked at the seller, he hissed at me, too. Everything in his stall was covered in snakeskin, including his staff, which had a copper snake's head on the handle.

"You're far from home," came a voice from the next stall.

I was starting to feel drunk with all the sights and sounds and strange things around me. Plus the drug dealer's pills had kicked in properly now, and my vision was fizzing at the edges.

"Is it that obvious?" I asked the man behind the counter. He had tufts of fur sprouting from his collar and sleeves, and his face was one large unibeard. He smelled like dog saliva and warm rocks, and freshly butchered meat.

"So are you," I said, and he laughed.

There's something about a werewolf laugh. It's contagious.

"I can help you find what you're looking for, if you like."

"I can't pay you," I said, and when he started to reply, I cut him off. "—and I don't want to owe a werewolf a favor."

He smiled at me, and his large canines shone under the glow of the fairy lights above. Now, I would warn people like Bron that you should under no circumstances ever accept a favor from a werewolf, but I was running out of time.

"I was just about to pack up, anyway," he said, looking up at the sky. I saw then that it was a full moon. "It's time for me to get out of here."

An extra tuft of brown fur grew out of the top of his hand as he packed his things, and he grew a few inches taller, but more stooped. He bunched up the pelts from his counter and tied them with string, then threw them into the gaping mouth of his bag on the ground.

"What are you looking for?" he asked, blinking his long eyelashes at me. The necklace of animal teeth around his neck clicked as he moved.

"Potions," I said.

"Ah, you won't have much trouble then. They're all over the market. Same potions, same prices. Like MacDonalds. There's one in this very lane, just a few stalls down. The ugliest troll you'll ever lay your eyes on. He calls himself Alchemist Larson, but really he's just a retired librarian. We call him Crooked Larry." The werewolf gave me a skew smile, but I didn't return it.

"Not just any potion," I said, and looked into his hungry brown eyes. He stopped packing, and straightened up. "Ah."

I smelt the forest leaves on his fur, and the blood. I could see he was thinking of lecturing me on how I shouldn't be at EverShade, shouldn't be talking to a werewolf, and certainly shouldn't be considering buying Council-banned substances, but then his nose twitched and he kept talking.

"Then you're looking for the Orc Enclave." He pointed north-east with two of his long, hairy fingers, crowned with dirty yellow claws. "They don't like to mix with us mud folk."

I wanted to give him something, but my pockets were empty.

"You don't owe me anything," he said, hopping on the spot, pulling his backpack onto his shoulders. He saluted me, and

I watched as the moonlight glinted on his downy back as he walked away.

THE ORC ENCLAVE was more like the SubRealm I knew, with barrel-chested orcs striding around, grunting at each other, and drinking *Orc Extra Lager*. I could hear Goblin Punk music as I approached, which made me think of the night the gang had gunned down The Orc Godfather. He had survived, just to die the next day at the hands of his wife, and left an entire nation of orcs feeling rudderless. You could feel it in the air. They had always been savage creatures, but now it was like they didn't have anyone to answer to, they could forget their inhibitions—which to be fair, were minimal in the first place—but it certainly made them more dangerous.

Everywhere I looked, I saw the Hammerskin logo, which sent my adrenaline spiking. The Khargol familia was vicious, murderous, and showed no mercy, but the Hammerskins made them look like the bloody Brady Bunch. The Hammerskins were Neo-Nazis with everything to prove. They had been rallying against Don Vito Or'Capone for decades, and now that he was sleeping with the fishes, they knew it was their chance to shine (*shine* being an operative word, in this case, because the standard orc is a revolting creature, and the only thing shiny about them are their backstreet orc-steel shivs, with which they would have no problem skewering you in the back).

In the main part of the black magic market I was able to blend in to a degree, because of the melting pot of cultures, but as I walked into the Orc Enclave I became an alien. I cursed myself again for not thinking ahead to bring the glamour potion. The orcs stopped and stared as I walked through their section, as if I were painted neon-pink. They laughed and sloshed beer over each other and whistled at me as I walked past, asking me if I was lost, and why I wasn't smiling. There's nothing quite as flattering as being catcalled by a table of drunk skinhead Neo-Nazi orcs.

I wended my way through the orcs that just seemed to be there to party, and moved toward the more serious looking guys. There were more beer stalls and food trucks there than in the general market, and the more business-like booths were in the shadows, at the rear. Trying to shake off the glares cutting into my back, I quickly surveyed the items on offer. Enchanted jewelry; "love potions" (I had a feeling this was just a horse tranquillizer, not unlike the one I had been drugged with when I was last in the SubRealm); magical wigs and self-tan, and Elvish Presley vests. When I got to the end of the row of stalls, which ended on a street, a motor-bike roared past, cutting me off.

Is that it? I thought, as I turned around and looked at the sellers again. I'll admit that I was rather disappointed by the lack of contraband goods on offer. And I didn't understand why they would risk coming to a verboten market to sell vests made in China when they could rather do it at a local (legal) flea market.

No, I was missing something. I was definitely missing something.

That's when I saw the motorbike again. There was a goblin parking it on the opposite end of the aisle of stalls. He pulled off his oversized white helmet and locked it away in the cubby, and put something small in the back pocket of his pants. As I watched, he took a few steps forward and opened an invisible curtain, stepped through, and disappeared. A portal within a portal.

This isn't EverShade, I realized. *Whatever's behind that curtain is EverShade.*

I hurried in the goblin's footsteps, found the curtain, and pulled it open. There seemed to be nothing there, but when I pushed my foot forward, it vanished. I took a breath and stepped through the portal.

CHAPTER 22

BLACK SYRUP

This was where that stink of evil was coming from. The air was thick with it, and I tried my best not to choke as it made its way up my nose and down my throat. It was eerie and disgusting, and made orc breath smell like roses on a fresh spring day. Even my eyes, protected by the sunglasses, began to water. How did they stand it? It was like working in a nail bar run by psychopaths. I took off the shades to wipe my face.

"Nano. Mask." I said, and my nano turned from a hood into a black mask that fitted my face perfectly. The mesh in front of my mouth didn't remove the taste of the black magic completely, but at least I could breathe without retching.

EverShade was a hungry black space. Black upon black upon black. The painkillers added just a hint of color, and it looked like I had the northern lights edging my vision. I felt more confident to move around with the mask covering my face, but the physical act of walking through the dark place was difficult, as if I had fingers holding me back. As if all the good magic inside me was rebelling and pulling me back from the inside, wanted me to leave. I could feel the presence of the Void all around me. Usually it seemed to be a happy and benevolent energy, but here it flickered with danger. I had to get out of this strange place as soon as possible.

The creatures here all wore black robes, and stalked about with their heads bowed, like depressed monks. There was minimal communication, nothing at all like the market I had just come from. Questions, answers, and money were all exchanged under a heavy blanket of hush. I walked up to the first table, which had no wares on display, and the man with a reptilian face looked at me, his scales shining in the dim light. His lizard face startled me, and I was doubly grateful for the mask, which hid my horrified expression. His thin red tongue shot out in my direction, smelling the air between us.

"You don't belong here," he hissed. "Spy." He looked around, probably wondering if he should announce it and have me lynched on the spot.

"No!" I said in a hard whisper. "Not a spy." I looked around too, hoping that no one had heard him speak.

He stared at me, his tongue darting. Trying to taste my essence, and my reason for being where I didn't belong.

"I need something," I said, and he just kept staring at me,

his beady lizard eyes not giving anything away. "Voodoo serum," I whispered. *"Spiritus Morbus."*

He stopped tonguing the air.

"Get lost, Wizard," he said, "or you'll be sorry you ever laid eyes on me."

To illustrate his threat, he opened his black robe to reveal a utility belt with various silver tools hanging from it. They looked like implements from a torturer's table: spikes, blades, pliers. I dragged my eyes away and did my best to get lost.

THE SITUATION FELT HOPELESS. I was far from home and totally out of my depth. I had dealt with evil before, mostly in the form of violent vampires, but in EverShade it felt like I was walking in black sinking sand. Every person I walked past had their own brand of maleficence, roiling like dark smoking haloes around their heads. I didn't know how I would find the serum, and I started thinking that being at the black magic market had been a terrible idea from beginning to end. I should have just told Willard that there was nothing I could do for Abarim. But then I thought of the old wizard screaming in his bed stained by sweat and blood, and I knew that I'd never be able to live with myself if I had just walked away.

· · ·

MY ENERGY BEGAN TO DISSIPATE, as if the market was drawing on my power. I watched the people in black robes milling around and I felt exceptionally tired and lonely, as if I'd never feel happiness again. The ground gave out a magnetic force, trying to pull me down to it. I kept walking through the black syrup, my light fading with every step. The evil stench had covered every part of me, and I felt it in my chest too, and my brain.

This place should come with a warning, I thought. *Like those cigarette boxes with pictures of diseased organs. Charcoal throat and inked lungs. This place gives you a starless heart.*

I caught sight of the goblin again, the one who had unknowingly shown me the way in. Maybe I was desperate, but I thought of him then as my lucky charm. I increased my pace, not wanting to let him disappear again. He was visiting various stalls, handing over gold coins and credit card slips, and receiving bags and boxes of products in return. I followed him, trying to hear what he was saying to the vendors.

"... it has to be there by one a.m., Zeel," said the proprietor, handing a black plastic bag over. There were no products on his table or on display behind him.

"No problem," said the goblin, looking at his watch. He scribbled in his small notebook, then tucked his pencil on top of his leathery ear. "I'll make it my first stop." The loot went into his carrier bag, and the book into the back pocket of his grubby jeans.

The goblin was a courier. A spark of hope lit my thoughts. I didn't need to find out who was selling the serum, all I needed was that little book.

I followed Zeel surreptitiously to his next stop, where an orc was skinning a small animal on his counter. It was a brutal sight. I had to avert my eyes, and in doing so I caught sight of the tattoo on his shoulder. He was a Hammerskin. The goblin didn't seem perturbed by the carcass at all.

"Zeel," grunted the orc, gesturing at the two small boxes beside him. "Two."

The goblin took out his book and grabbed his pencil, noting down the addresses, then leaned over the bleeding pink flesh on the counter to grab the parcels waiting for him. As before, his pencil went behind his ear, his book into his back pocket. As he left the Hammerskin stall I made sure I was right behind him, but not too close to alert him to my presence. I unclipped my wand and held it under my coat.

Perfect place to pickpocket.

I sensed that I had to be very careful, using magic in that place. There was so much of the dark stuff swirling around that it would be easy to make a mistake. My grip tightened on my mother's wand. I spoke under my breath, barely loud enough to hear it myself. As Zeel slowed to approach the next counter, I said *"Volas,"* and the notebook eased out of the goblin's pocket and floated up in the air. I grabbed it on my way past, pocketed it, and ducked into the next aisle, walking back to the portal as quickly as I could without bringing attention to myself. At the opposite end of the market I found the lizard-man's stall, then the gateway. I wrenched the invisible curtains aside, stepping up and out into the Orc Enclave, which was rowdier than before. My heart thumped hard against my ribs as I walked past Zeel's stationary motorbike, past the drunken catcallers, and back to the cobblestoned night market.

CHAPTER 23

BURIED

S pending those nights on the street when I was a kid were the hardest years of my life. I remember the hunger, the cold, the bitter ashy sour stink of us Ferals. The way people used to look at us, as if we were something they wanted to scrape off their shoes. I learned some important lessons from the Ferals, but the knowledge I value most is the quick and dirty magic they taught me. Specifically, how to pick pockets. I pulled my trench coat tighter around me as I walked back through the night market, beneath the fairy lights. I bee-lined for the old wooden trolley in the dark corner, where Lou had delivered me, but I couldn't find any way to open the portal. I scraped my hand black on the dirty bricks, trying to find the silver handle.

"Deodamnatus," I swore, hitting the wall in frustration, then leaning against it. I pushed the mask up, off my face, so that I could breathe properly. Zeel would already have noticed

his notebook was missing, and I didn't want to be around when the Dark Arts suppliers got wind of what had happened. I pounded on the wall again, but it stubbornly remained bricks and mortar. Then a shadow grew over it.

"We meet again," said a smooth voice from behind me.

I spun around. It was the tall, awkward woman with the plastic face and blunt-cut blond wig. As I watched, she curled her fingers under the wig and pulled it off, and her mask peeled off with it. It was the vampire with the cheek-bones. Blondie.

"Hello," he said. "What a happy coincidence."

Not happy, I thought. *Not a coincidence.*

"You should have left that glamour on," I said. "It was an improvement."

He smirked. We both knew it wasn't true.

"You've been following me," I said.

"You've been fun to watch."

I stood on my tip-toes and glanced behind him. There was some activity in the Enclave. Some people talking in raised voices.

He looked over his shoulder. "There seems to be some commotion down there."

I blinked at him, innocently, then shrugged.

Blondie's eyes drilled into mine. "You don't perhaps have something tucked away in that coat of yours, do you? Something that doesn't belong to you?"

"None of your business," I said.

"Don't you know that this portal closes at midnight?" he asked.

What was this? I thought. *A warped version of Cinderella? No, I did not know that the portal closed at midnight. I've never been to an illegal night market before. But with any luck, this irritating vampire would turn into a pumpkin. If he knew anything about my days at the Copperfield Institute, he'd know that pumpkins make the best targets for archery practice.*

"They'll be here in minutes," he said. "They'll eat you alive. Do you know what they do to people like you?"

An ice-cube ran down my back. I swallowed hard. The brick wall that I had backed up against felt as solid as ever.

"I should just ash you right now," I said. "That would stop you from showing up at inconvenient times."

The ruckus was getting louder.

"But if you did that," said the vampire, "I wouldn't be able to get you out of here."

I choked on a laugh. "You?" I said. "Do you think I would go anywhere with you? A *vampire*?"

There was shouting coming from behind him, tables being kicked over, lights torn down. A whirlwind of malicious energy that threatened to mow us down, too.

"It doesn't look like you have much of a choice," he said, looking back again.

My brain whirred in panic. "You'd take me somewhere worse than this."

"That's not a nice way to describe your apartment," he said, a smile quirking his lips.

"You'll take me home?"

"I'll take you wherever you want to go."

"I don't believe you."

"Scouts' honor," he said. He knew better than to say *vampires' honor,* because he knew it didn't exist.

There was absolutely no way I was going to willingly go anywhere with a vampire. No way, not a chance in hell.

Not. Gonna. Happen.

"Jax," he said urgently. "They're coming for you."

I looked behind him again, and this time I spotted the reptilian face, and he saw me at the same time, and shouted out, then strode toward us, his weapons of torture bouncing off his thighs and glinting in the light. Fear dissolved my insides, and I looked up at Blondie.

Better the devil you know, right?

"Okay," I said, every syllable hurting me. "Please help me."

The vampire pulled my body down to the greasy cobble-stones and threw his cape over me.

"Ianua Sit," he said, then tightened his grip, hurting my shoulder as he squeezed. I let out a sharp exhalation, but then the pain disappeared with a flash of light as we fell between the stones and tumbled through the air, then slid in the dark so fast that I couldn't catch my breath.

WHEN I WOKE UP, I was in a comfortable chair, in a cozy lounge that I didn't recognize. Classical music played through an invisible sound system. The room was warm, the light was dim, and the finishings were stylish and expensive. It was certainly not my apartment.

Blondie appeared, a tumbler of water in each hand. I reached for my wand, but it was gone. My crossbow was at home. I had one arm to defend myself with.

"Where am I?" I asked. "Where's my wand?"

He passed me one of the glasses of water, and I smacked it out of his hand, ready to hear it smash on the expensive looking floor. Instead, it paused before it hit the ground, and the water that had splashed out of it wobbled in the air, then made its way back into the tumbler, which flew back into Blondie's palm.

"Shall we try that again?" he said. "I'm sure you must be thirsty."

I was thirsty. I felt as if I had been walking in a desert for a week with only salt and vinegar crisps for company. He held it out to me again, and I shook my head. I had already accepted way too many favors from way too many dangerous creatures that night.

"Where's my wand?"

"I'll give it back to you," he said. "I just didn't want you to ash me here in my own sitting room."

I stared at him.

"Just had the carpets done," he said, and smiled.

I didn't smile back. "You said you'd portal me home."

"I said I'd take you wherever you wanted to go. You didn't have time to give me an address."

"So you brought me here. How convenient."

"The offer still stands. I'll take you wherever you want to go. But—"

"Yes," I said. "I was waiting for the *but*."

"But we have something to discuss, first."

"Of course we do," I said, kicking the glass coffee table with my mucky boots.

The vampire stared at me. "You could show some gratitude, you know."

"For kidnapping me?"

"For saving your life. You have no idea what they would have done to you."

I remembered the reptilian's flicking tongue, his glinting tools.

"What are we going to talk about?" I asked.

Blondie laughed. "There's only one thing we need from you, Jacquelyn Denna Knight, and you know what it is."

Frustration tore through my brain and I kicked the table again, hurting my toes. "I told you I don't have the HighFire Crown!"

"But you'll find it for us," he said.

It was my turn to laugh. "No. That crown is molten lava, Vampire. Molten lava in a volcano pocket realm that doesn't even exist anymore. So, no. I'm not going to find it. And if, by some miracle, I did, I certainly wouldn't be handing it over to vampires."

He angled his head and gazed at me, thinking. "Nothing I say will convince you?"

I thought of his promises of my personal file. My parents' names, the address of our family home, my own real surname that was lost to me. I wanted the information so badly that my insides ached.

"Can you just tell me one thing?" I asked. "Just one thing I don't know?" Then I cleared my throat and tried to take the desperation out of my voice. "Just so that I know you're not lying about the file?"

Blondie stared at me a while longer, thinking. "Okay," he said.

My lungs swelled.

"What do you want to know?"

A hundred shouting questions elbowed each other to get to the front of the queue. I wanted to know the answers to all of them, I was desperate to know everything about the life that was snatched away from me. I thought of the Belore funeral: the rampant green grass, the magical oaks, the hungry holes in the ground.

I cleared my throat again. "I want to know where my parents are buried."

The vampire did little to hide the surprise on his face. He took a few moments, frowning, and pushed his hair out of his face. Then he looked at me. "You think they were *buried?*"

CHAPTER 24

A VAMPIRE'S PITY

It was a difficult choice to pick the address I wanted Blondie to deliver me to. His portal magic was impressive, and I couldn't help feeling a begrudging admiration for his spell casting. Usually I didn't like the fact that vampires could sling spells, but his elegant casting was most certainly the only reason I was breathing, so I guess I was re-evaluating my standpoint on that, even if it twisted my guts.

Blondie—whose real name, he told me, is Lysander—had given me back my wand after I had started weeping. I wasn't proud of the fact that I had broken down completely in the middle of a vampire's sitting room, but it had been a long day, and the mention of my parents had cut me to the quick. I had always pictured my parents lying peacefully in their graves in a beautiful enchanted wizard cemetery, but now I knew this was just a childish fantasy. Of course that scarred vampire in the corner of their bedroom, that killer, had not left their bodies there. Why would he? No. He'd take the evidence with him, to get rid of it. How? It was one of the few details I didn't want to know. The grief that lies inside me—that will forever lie inside me—stretched and howled, and I howled along with it, causing Lysander to take pity on me. A vampire's pity! What had my life come to? It only made me weep louder.

Lysander gave me back my wand and reiterated the deal. The file, in exchange for the Crown.

"Try to stay alive till then," he joked, which actually made me stop crying. Not because it was funny, but because I understood that if the vampires thought I was the only one who would be able to find the HighFire Crown, then they would want to keep me alive. That's why Lysander spared my life—twice—and that's why he was, by all appearances, helping me.

But I saw the big picture, and I wouldn't be taken in by extremely good-looking vampires who seemed to be making a habit of saving my bacon. I refused to be lulled into a false sense of security. Lysander didn't care about *me*, he cared about the Crown, which I suspected was the missing piece of the puzzle for the Silvano Clan's mission to take over the Realm. And if that happened, I was as good as dead, as were the rest of the sworn enemies of the Silvanos—which numbered in the hundreds—and included Ferra's whole family, the Belore twins, and Darick.

. . .

When Lysander asked me where I wanted to go, it wasn't an easy decision. There were four different places I needed to be: home, for a well-deserved rest. A doctor, to get regular-strength legal painkillers that didn't make me see the northern lights at the edge of my vision. *The Olde Worlde Railway* station, to protect Tambo Vuleka and the starry-eyed tourists... and the address I had found in the goblin courier's delivery notebook. His handwriting was abysmal, but I managed to find exactly what I was looking for. It was dated a couple of weeks before.

2 oz SPIRITUS MORBUS V/S, it said. S ABARIM. 106 MERLIN DRIVE. ORANGE GROVE.

If I hadn't almost died getting that damn notebook—and probably lost years of my life—I would have said that it was too easy, that the address was just scrawled out like that. Then I remembered Lou's rough portaling magic, not being able to breathe under the black bag over my head, the crazy gypsy woman, the werewolf, the Hammerskins, the creepy reptilian, the black syrup, and being kidnapped by a vampire. It hadn't been easy at all.

I gave the address to Lysander, who had made good on his promise, and had transported me through a sparking gray tunnel to arrive right outside Blimaex Abarim's brother's house.

· · ·

It was large, sprawling, and post-apocalyptic-looking from the outside. It was everything Blimaex's house was, but turned upside down and dipped in evil. The timber cladding was rotting and falling away, the garden was a jungle of spiky weeds and nettles, which I only learned as I made my way up the path, because it was past midnight and I had lost Lou's night-vision shades somewhere in EverShade. The plant stung me on my good hand; stung me as if it had a personal vendetta against me. As if I had taken out its entire family, and this was its one and only chance to seek vengeance. The spiteful plant's poison crackled against my skin, and sent a sharp, shooting pain up my arm. Stones tripped me in the dark, and blackjacks jumped on to my clothes like hungry fleas.

I got the message loud and clear: I was not welcome.

I crept up the rotting steps toward the front door, which was padlocked with an old rusty mechanism. Only the 0 of the 106 house number remained on the wall.

"Rumpis," I whispered, and the padlock crumbled easily in my hands. It had only needed a hint of destructive energy to fall apart.

I put my hand on the door, ready to push it open. I hesitated. Was I really going to break into the house of a wizard who had turned to the dark side? I was lucky to be alive, after the kind of day I had experienced. As I pushed the door open I had a horrible feeling that my luck was about to run out.

CHAPTER 25

A FLICK OF THE WRIST

The door creaked as I opened it. Of course it did. Slyden Abarim's house was like the epitomic haunted house of your worst night terrors. But it wasn't haunted in the happy way that my apartment was, with a cheerful ghost who plays tricks on me and does my laundry. This house wasn't haunted by a specter but by the evil deeds the wizard had performed. The Dark Arts have a way of following you around in everything you do. It's not something you dabble with at breakfast time and by dinner your hands are clean. It latches onto you with its dirty barbs, claws into your skin, sinks into your flesh and stains your skeleton.

Dark Bone, Directress Copperfield had said to us in the classroom that day, her titanium hair glinting in the light. Everything about this house was dark. No wonder someone like Slyden felt comfortable among the creatures at EverShade.

He was one of them, and his house was an extension of that evil.

I made my way slowly and carefully through the front entrance hall, resisting the urge to light my wand. Even in the dark I could make out how dirty and dilapidated the interior was. Rats squeaked and scurried, smells of decay wrapped around me, and plates of half-eaten food squirmed with maggots. Sour liquid bubbled in my throat and I had to fight to keep it down. I had to stop moving, close my eyes, and focus on not throwing up. That's when I heard the incantation, like the buzz of a giant fly, coming from the room upstairs, which was framed by the softest flickering of candlelight. My stomach turned to stone.

Slyden was awake, and he was making magic. The mumbling had a fury to it, an urgency, and my bet was that he was trying to finish his brother off. My anger started to simmer in my chest. I wasn't lucky enough to have siblings, and I craved the connection I was denied, especially when my parents were killed. But this old wizard thought it was okay to not only torment his own kin, but his own flesh-and-blood brother. It was time for someone to stop him.

I climbed the stairs, my anger and purpose driving my limbs, making me forget how tired my legs were. The pain in my shoulder faded to background static. I unclipped the wand from my belt and ran through the spells I would employ to debilitate the man. I tried to control my breathing, which was terse; tried to keep my heart from hammering. A dark wizard can kill you with a flick of the wrist. I needed to go in fast and hard, and hope that the element of surprise would give me the edge over his power.

The buzzing got louder, and now I could make out some words, a few of which I recognized, and they made me feel chilled. If that incantation was directed at his brother, Blimaex would surely be dead. I imagined him dying as I stood there, outside Slyden's room. Imagined Willard fussing around him, offering his water and changing his sheets, knowing all the while that none of it mattered. Not anymore.

I took a deep, silent breath, and held my wand fast. I allowed the anger and sadness in my chest to boil up, into my throat and down my arms, until I felt as if I was glowing. I swept up all the power I was gathering and forced it through my left arm and into my wand as I turned the corner. *"Ignem Exquiris!"* I yelled, and the hot blue lightning bolted out of my wand and into the room, in the direction of the black-robed wizard standing in the center.

The electricity slammed into him, and I watched his chalky face and black eyes as he stared at me, stared right into my soul.

"Ignem Exquiris!" I yelled again, and another shot of current sliced into him. He kept staring, and I hated it, hated how it felt on my skin, as if he was stealing something from me. My left arm wasn't as strong as my right, and two lightning spells was enough to burn it out. I wrenched my right arm

from the *The Cure* sling and caught my wand with my stronger hand.

"Glaciem Exquiris!" I shouted, and I compelled the fear inside me to turn to ice and to flow through my wand and into Slyden Abarim, who was still drinking in my eyes and my skin. A stream of ice shot out of my wand and speared the wizard in the chest.

Got him! I thought. *Got him!*

But he ignored the icicle lodged in his chest. He was still standing, and staring.

"Rumpis!" I shouted. *Destroy!* There was a crashing, and gray smoke. But still, he stood.

I would have to use the Death Spell, I thought. It's not a spell I ever liked using; it was temperamental and extremely dangerous, especially when used on a more powerful wizard, but none of my elemental magic was working. I gathered my courage, and held my wand out. It's not easy to sling a spell that you know may very well be your last.

I began the chant, but stopped when I noticed that Slyden hadn't said anything, or done anything to protect himself. He hadn't moved a muscle. I looked at his face again and felt his eyes drilling into me. *What was going on?*

By then, it was too late. I stepped forward and understood that it wasn't a wizard at all, but a chimera. I spun around to face the doorway I had just stepped through, and the real Slyden Abarim was standing there. He towered over me, his black-veined, bloodless face peering out from his hood, his eyes dead marbles, shining black. He lifted his ebony staff and whipped a black whirlwind of silk ribbon around me, binding my body, my eyes, and my mouth. My wand clattered to the floor as I fell, immobilized, and Slyden grabbed my feet and began to drag me downstairs.

CHAPTER 26

GRAVEYARD SOIL UNDER MY NAILS

Slyden Abarim dragged me by the feet down the stairs, and every bump sent a bright blue flash of pain through me. He trawled my body through his filthy, cockroach-infested house, and just when I thought it couldn't get worse, I heard the *thunk* of a heavy trapdoor being opened, and, with rasping breath, he pulled me down another flight of concrete steps, into his basement, where the walls were so thick that our sounds—my groaning, his breathing—seemed exaggerated, and the world outside was completely muted. Only a sliver of light made its way through the ribbon over my eyes, and it was moving. I guessed it was a naked lightbulb, swinging from the low ceiling.

Then there was a nerve-grating crashing sound, and I flinched. It was a wire cage being forcefully opened. Slyden threw me into it, and the wire dug into my skin. The cage was large enough to pull myself up into a sitting position, but not high enough to stand. It reminded me of the cages at the Reef Hall in the SubRealm which had contained the magical animals the orcs used to bait in their savage cage fights.

This time I was the magical creature in the cage, except that my arms were bound to my sides and my wand was upstairs in Slyden's sorcery room. There wouldn't be a lot of magic bouncing off these walls. I heard the cage being locked, and Slyden's footsteps retreat. Then he climbed the stairs and banged the trapdoor shut.

I allowed myself one minute's rest, my head leaning against the back of the cage, then it was time to get to work. I wasn't panicking... yet. I had been in this position before, in the Obsidian Hill Cemetery, when a giant spiderweb had seemingly come alive and decided to stitch me up and embroider me to death, almost suffocating me in the process. I had cut my way out of that cursed cocoon, and I'd be able to cut myself out of this silk, too.

I took a few deep breaths, trying to calm my heart, which was doing tumble turns in my chest. With every breath, I slowed my body and my mind, until it was a still pond, and I was able to focus. I was wand-less and my mouth was gagged, so I needed laser focus to make the spell work. I allowed the fear to come forward and wash over me: fear of what Slyden planned to do to me; fear of what had happened to Blimaex; fear of being kept down here in this creepy basement forever. The fear rushed through my body and I directed it to my fingers.

Ignem Exquiris, I thought, as clearly as I could.

I expected the fear to burst from my fingers in the form of hot lasers, and cut open the ribbon binding as it had the spider's silk, but it did not. The magic stopped at my hands, and refused to leave my body.

Ignem Exquiris, I thought again, and felt the heat in my fingers again, but the magic was not unleashed.

Ventum Exquiris! I thought. Nothing, not even a breeze.

Contendis!

Crickets.

Metaphorical tumbleweed rolled through the room.

My magic wasn't working.

Then the gravity of my situation began to sink in. Slyden, that evil *fillius canis,* had placed some kind of enchantment on his basement. Some kind of barrier, so that I couldn't access the energy of the Void; so that every spell I tried to sling was dead in the water. All the work I had done in calming my body fell away as I broke into a cold sweat and fresh adrenaline zinged through my veins. That's when I heard the squeaking, and the stomach-turning squelching, of the rats that had come out to play.

I SCREAMED into my gag and tried to kick at them, but my legs were bound as tightly as the rest of my body. Despite my bucking and flailing, I was not a threat. They advanced steadily, and I could hear their hungry shrieks and clacking teeth as they climbed on top of me and stuck their whiskers into the crook of my elbows, my neck, my ears.

Nano. Helmet! I thought, but the nano was stuck in my pocket, unable to slip out to transform. Even if it could escape, the magic it relied on to work had been cut off by Slyden. I felt a pinch on my hand as one of the creatures took a bite, and I shouted and kicked again, dislodging some of them. But I had a feeling they hadn't eaten in a long time, and they saw me as the feast they had been dreaming of. They wasted no time in scrambling back on, nipping and squeaking and scratching at me with their stabbing needles of contaminated claws.

I thought again of the night I spent at Obsidian. Without wanting to, I remembered finding Ametrix Belore's decomposing body in the timber chest, shredded by rats. The picture of his destroyed face flashed in on me in graphic detail. I cried out, as if I was still there in the cemetery, with graveyard soil under my nails. This time I couldn't stop the vomit that lurched out of me, but the gag held it back, choking me. I couldn't get any air. The bile went into my lungs and my sinuses, and I coughed and struggled against the gag, drowning in my own vomit as the rats danced on my shuddering body.

HEAVING, trying to drag air into my lungs, I scraped my face against the bottom of the cage with all the strength I had, trying to dislodge the gag so that I could breathe. My lungs were on fire, my cheek was raw and bleeding, but I didn't care. All I needed was air. I didn't even care about the rats anymore, didn't care that they were all over me and partying like it was 1999. The only thing I cared about was the next breath, and as my lungs screamed I started to think I would never breathe again. My body began to give up. It collapsed one limb at a time, until I was lying face-down on the bottom of the cage, my head throbbing, my eyes bulging. My thoughts faded, my consciousness shrank to a small blip.

I held on. Despite my body surrendering, despite my starving organs, I held on to that tiny blip, that tiny flame of consciousness, because it was all I had left. I knew that if that light went out, I'd be a goner, and the next breath I'd take would be an abstract one, in the Underworld, in my Halloween Heaven, which I'm sure is a lot less sweet than it sounds.

One of the rats plopped his warm bundle of fur behind my ear, and started chewing my nape. I didn't shake him off. I kept my eye on the small flame, and kept it burning.

My lungs stopped screaming.

There was quiet; a beautiful quiet that cascaded over my silk-bound body, and the dark basement disappeared, and the cage disappeared. I didn't let myself swim in the direction of the dark portal that had opened up—the gateway that was promising me peace—but I floated toward it, anyway.

Just as I felt my body falling away—or my spirit lifting up, I wasn't sure which—the gag fell off, slamming me back to earth. I was able to suck in deep, shuddering breaths, and the light returned to my mind. Slowly at first, almost reluctantly, then in a bright beam that promised me I was going to live to fight another day. The rat had chewed through the binding that had been suffocating me, perforating it. As I tried to stretch my arms, the enchanted ribbon tore.

I'm free, I thought, relief and pain mixing together. I turned onto my back and wiped the vomit from my mouth with my sleeve.

I'm free.

But then I opened my eyes and saw the top of the cage, which I had forgotten about in my flailing to live. I was still in a locked cage in a locked basement. Not just an ordinary basement, mind you, but a cellar that had snuffed out my magic. I began to shiver wildly. I was in shock, and I was cold, and alone. The darkness inside me swirled up, and as I eyed the sniffing rodents that surrounded me I wondered if they had done me a favor by saving my life, or if they had only served to extend my torture.

CHAPTER 27

THE PERKS OF PURGATORY

I gritted my teeth and forced myself to count my blessings. I was breathing. I still had my fingers and my toes, my nano and my coat. Most importantly, I had my mind, and it was strong, and clear, and I was going to find my way out of this basement.

I inspected the lock on the cage. It was a small steel contraption, and wouldn't have stood a chance with my *Rumpis* spell, if only I was able to cast it. I wondered why Slyden had a cage down here, anyway, and what kinds of things he kept in it, or planned to keep in it, and it sent a chill down my spine. The picture of Blimaex's brother that I had in my head when I had first learned of his existence was a kind of neutral wizard who had just dabbled in the Dark Arts and been punished for it accordingly, cut out of the well-regarded family, and out of the will. But that's not the wizard I met today—and I use the term "met" loosely—this man had lost his way completely. He was so immersed in his dark world that everything else had ceased to matter. I couldn't get the picture of him out of my head: his lunar skin, his dead black-as-abyss eyes. Slyden was pure evil, and I was his prisoner.

I sat in the corner of the cage and tried to think of an escape plan. My body was recovering from the trauma, and as the shock receded, the pain arrived, crashing in waves over me. I winced as I massaged my swollen shoulder, which had not benefited from being dragged down two flights of concrete steps. I felt in my pocket for the painkillers I got from Lou, and shook two capsules into my palm. My mouth was drier than a desert desiccant, but I forced the pills down anyway. I'd need them if I was going to go hand-to-hand with Slyden.

I shook the top of the cage to test the lock, inadvertently startling the rats. The lock didn't give.

"Sorry," I said to the rodents, and they just sniffed the air and twitched their whiskers.

I sat back again, leaning against the metal wire. I had to admit, the situation was looking a little hopeless, but I had never let that stop me before. There was a way out, I just needed to find it.

The drugs started kicking in, and a lovely warm ripple of pain relief washed over my injured shoulder. I don't know why I had wanted to go to a regular doctor for regular painkillers when I had these, which were much, much better. They didn't just take away the pain of my shoulder;

my whole ransacked body began to feel better, and then the northern lights appeared again at the edges of my vision, and it felt good. I rested against the mesh and closed my eyes while I let the pharma work its magic.

"You're in quite the pickle," said a woman's voice.

I flinched, and my eyes clicked open.

What the hell? Was there someone else down here? Another one of Abarim's prisoners?

I looked around the dark recesses of the room, my head moving in jerky movements.

"Hello?" I said.

"Hello," she said, and there she was, right in front of me. Sitting on an imaginary table, and swinging her black latex-covered legs. It was Liz Durison, dressed as a dominatrix. Or, rather, it was the ghost of Liz Durison, dressed as a dominatrix.

"Liz," I said, blinking. *These pills are* strong.

"That's me," she said, twirling her whip. "I'm surprised you remember my name."

Remember your name? I thought. *Your name is engraved into every day. Your face is what I see when I drift off into a fitful sleep, and it's there in the twilight hours when I toss and turn. I wouldn't be able to forget your face if I tried.*

"Of course I remember your name," I said. "I'm trying to solve your murder."

She made a surprised face. "Are you?"

"Yes," I said.

"That's funny," she said, adjusting her stiletto. "Because I've been watching you, and I don't think you're trying very hard."

"I am," I said. "I've just had some other fires to put out along the way."

Liz laughed and looked around at the bleak basement walls, then looked at me in an intense way. "You don't understand."

"Understand what?" I asked.

She yanked her bustier open to show me the branded symbol on her chest. "You don't understand how important it is that you find the people who did this to me."

I remembered Durison's naked body, dead skin like wax.

"I will find the people who did it," I said. "I'm trying my best."

"Try harder!" she shouted, whipping the table, the snapping sound making me jump.

"I went to your house today," I said.

"I know," she said. "I was there."

"I was looking for the first domino."

"And you found it," she said. "Damn it. You found it."

I looked up at her, frowning. "Did I?"

"Do you need me to spell it out for you?"

"Well," I said. "Seeing as you offered. That would be very helpful."

She had a disgusted look on her face. "You know it doesn't work like that."

She clicked her fingers, and a glass of rosé appeared in her hand. She chugged it down, then clicked again for a refill.

"What?" she snapped, when she saw me staring. "Believe me, it's one of the very few perks of being stuck in purgatory."

"How *does* it work?" I asked. I had experience with vampires, werewolves, shape-shifters, goblins, elves, and fae. But I'd never had a ghost sit down and chat with me like this, drinking pink wine, as if we were at a bookclub. In someone's creepy basement.

Liz rolled her eyes so far back I worried she might lose them altogether. "Damn it!" she said again. "What am I working with, here? I thought you were supposed to be the best occult detective in the city!"

"I prefer *paranormal private-eye*," I said. I was going to say that it's the alliteration I like, but I changed my mind.

Durison and I were hardly on confessional terms, and I had questions for her.

"Damn it!" she shouted again, jumping off the table and throwing her glass against the wall, smashing it to pieces. The rats squeaked and scuttled for safety.

"I know you must be angry," I said. "I would be, too."

"Angry?" she seethed. "Angry?"

"Is there anything you can tell me about what happened? About what they did to you?"

"No," she said, stalking across the room and then back again. "Don't you think I would have told you that?"

"I don't know," I said.

Was I hallucinating from the shock of my earlier trauma, mixed with horse-strength painkillers, or was this really Liz's ghost, coming to haunt (or help) me?

"I knew it," snarled Durison. "I knew the second I laid eyes on you at Morgan's neighborhood barbecue. You're a charlatan. You're a fraud."

"I'm not," I said.

She laughed, and the bitter sound reverberated off the dank walls. "You call yourself a wizard. You're nothing but a deadbeat. Worse than that. You're a con artist."

And you're nothing but a bitch, I thought. *No wonder you needed a dating app to meet men.*

. . .

Liz stopped snarling, stopped moving, and looked me straight in the eye, then she disappeared like the picture on the TV when you pull the plug.

Was it something I said?

My mind flashed back to when I was on the Goblin City Hotel computer and I saw that scented sticky-note stuck onto the frame. *HobNob,* it said. The dating app for goblins. It had bothered me, and I wasn't sure why. I thought maybe, especially after inadvertently witnessing Polkadot and KandyKane's bonking olympics that perhaps I was just put out because it seemed like everyone was dating except me.

The reason it was bothering me was because it was a flashing red light, a clue to the V-Cult killer case.

You found it, Liz had said.

I scrabbled in the pocket of my coat for Durison's little black book which I had nicked from her S&M chamber at her house. I flipped to the last page of entries.

Shining_Knight *(4 stars)*

HotBloodedBear *(1 star)*

Rednasyl *(5! stars)*

. . .

THESE WEREN'T men's names, these were usernames from a dating app. Liz was arranging all of her booty calls online. Of course she was. She had a full time job and two kids to look after as a single mom. She didn't have time to hang out at seedy bars trying to pick up casual lovers. She was into S&M; she liked to be in control. Online dating suited her needs perfectly. *HobNob* was the goblin app, what was the untouched human app? I looked down at the book again, then paged to the front. Written in the softest pencil, on the front page, was the word FLINT.

There was a flurry of images in my head as things clicked into place. The other murdered women were also single, and my guess is that they were all using the same app.

The V-Cult killers were finding their targets via *Flint*. It was perfect for them: not only could they target single women, but they could target women who fitted the exact profile they were looking for. 5'8; athletic build; dark hair. All the details were laid bare; all you needed was a *Flint* profile and an internet connection. And if they had a profile we could connect to the murdered women, we'd find our killers.

Exhilarated, I leaned back and looked at the ceiling and the naked lightbulb. Finally, I had a way forward. But then my eyes focused on the metal wire of the cage and I felt so frustrated that I lost my temper. I thought I might know how to find the killers, but I was stuck there, and the idea of someone else being murdered in cold blood while I languished in an evil basement made me lash out. I punched the cage, kicked the lid, smashed the sides (and almost smashed my bones doing it). Usually when I lose my temper, I lose control of my magic, too, but my magic had been snuffed out, which made me even angrier. And then I stopped dead, mid-tantrum, panting.

I couldn't use my magic, *but could I use someone else's?*

I put Durison's Flint book back into my infinity pocket and brought out the new potion I had bought—then promptly forgotten about—at *Mason & Sons.* The small bottle of inhalant called *Nebulam*: a magic potion that can force a vapor spell.

CHAPTER 28

NEBULAM

I didn't waste any time. I twisted the cap off the small plastic bottle of *Nebulam* and pushed it up my nose, squirting the potion into both nostrils as if my life depended on it. I didn't have to wait long before I started to hear and feel the rushing in my head, and in my fingers and toes, like ice-water pins and needles. I wondered, too late, if the potion might not play well with the industrial strength painkillers I had taken earlier. The rushing got louder and louder till it was all I could hear, and I felt as if I was being smashed by arctic ocean waves, over and over, until one of the waves lifted me up. Then I was right out of the water and flying through the air, as if my spirit had left my body in that cage, except when I looked down, the cage was empty. I floated up to the ceiling, then to the stairs, and I streamed through the keyhole of the locked cellar door and into the downstairs portion of Slyden Abarim's house. I floated past the mess and up the stairs to his sorcery chamber, where his light was still on. This time it was the real Slyden sitting at his desk. The apparition he had created to fool me earlier was gone. As vapor I entered the room and watched him work. He was painting a voodoo doll with a bottle of clear liquid, which I assumed was the *Spiritus Morbus*. The doll looked like Blimaex, and had real hair glued to his scalp and chin. The stench of evil flowed from his black robes like black fog.

I drifted down toward the dirty carpet to where I had lost my wand. When the wizard had tied me up, I had dropped it, and it had rolled beneath the old wooden dresser in which I assumed Slyden kept his potion ingredients and assorted knick-knacks. I drifted down until I caught sight of it, then lay on the floor, out of Slyden's view, until I morphed back into my human form. I lay on the floor, catching my breath as quietly as I could. Then I reached slowly and soundlessly for the wand and picked it up. Slyden coughed, which made me flinch and almost drop it, but my grip remained steady. All my focus was on controlling my breathing, and gripping the wand. Despite inhaling the muck of the carpet and the stink of the old wizard's dirty slippers, I was in an excellent position to do some damage. Slyden couldn't see me, but I had a clear and unobstructed view of his wide open legs, and, more importantly, his crotch.

I whipped up all the emotion I had felt while I had been locked downstairs in the cage. The fear of the rats, the vomit that I almost drowned in, the pain of trying to smash open the cage. It was all right there, the feeling, and it was so intense it felt like I was glowing with it, that my organs had taken on a radioactive neon green. My wand started vibrating with the potential energy it was picking up from my body. I whipped up the energy some more, until I couldn't stand the buzzing, glowing sensation anymore, until it threatened to blind me, or burst out of me, or both. I harnessed the pain like the wild animal it was and then forced it out of my body: a raging current that was black when it was inside me but the wand focused the energy into a clear blue stream of lightning.

Fiat Fulgar!

The fiery flare of light bolted right for its target: Slyden Abarim's tackle.

As THE SPELL speared the old wizard in his balls, electrocuting him in the most painful way possible, he screamed and fell backwards in his chair. My hand was burning; it was by far the most potent lightning spell I had ever cast. I'd never felt anything like it. I stared at the blackened skin on my hand. My wand was incandescent. I smelt singed hair and cooked flesh, and I tried not to think about it. I wasn't there to show mercy, I was there to finish him off. I stepped forward, wand burning in my hand, and looked over the desk. Slyden was curled up in the fetal position, hands on his toolbox—or where his toolbox used to be—and whimpering like a soccer player. He looked frail, and old, but I refused to feel sorry for him. He didn't deserve my sympathy. He didn't deserve anything but to die right there, weeping into his smelly, stained rug.

I noticed, then, the medical fang lying on his table, and some plastic tubing snaking out of a small white cooler box. My mind couldn't make sense of the paraphernalia.

Why would Slyden be siphoning his own blood?

My hand couldn't handle another bolt of lightning, so I was considering shooting a dagger of ice into his curved back to finish him off, but his screaming was so loud it reverberated in my head and tangled my thoughts.

Deodamnatus, I thought, my wand cooling in my hand.

I understood I couldn't kill him; couldn't kill an old man writhing on the floor. I would let the Council deal with him. I retrieved my phone with shaking hands and sent the Council an emergency Hotline alert with Slyden's address. Out of the dead-zone of the basement, my phone jumped to life and dozens of messages came through, one after the other. I scooped the intricately carved voodoo doll of Blimaex off Slyden's desk and pocketed it, making sure it was safe. I considered smashing the bottle of *Spiritus Morbus* against the wall, *a la* Liz Durison, and watching the brown glass splinter, but a dark whisper made me slip it into my pocket instead.

With the residual emotion in my chest, I pointed my wand at Slyden again and said *"Impedio!"*, freezing him in his curled-up pose. Then using as much care as he had with me, I dragged him, via a *contendis* spell, out of the chamber and down the two flights of stairs, his head banging on every concrete step on the way down.

The rats in the basement greeted me like an old friend, squeaking and cleaning their whiskers. The room was still cutting off my magic, so I had to physically drag the wizard's frozen body down the last few stairs. Unfortunately I couldn't get him into the cage, but as I turned the key on the trapdoor I thought that, cage or no cage, he was wounded and locked in a magic-free basement, and he wasn't going anywhere anytime soon.

STILL SHAKING, I phoned Morgan, who answered on the first ring.

"Are you okay?" she demanded. "I've been trying to call you for hours but your phone was off."

"Sorry," I said, looking over at the trapdoor. "I didn't have any signal."

"There's a woman missing," she said, and I swung around and kicked the crumbling wall, swearing in the dirtiest Latin I could think of.

"Fits your description," she said. "Exactly like the others."

"Was she on *Flint*?" I asked.

"What?"

"*Flint.* That online dating app," I said.

"I don't know."

"Do you have access to her phone? Check her phone."

"Okay."

"Check everyone's phones, all the victims. Or their laptops."

"Slow down, Jax," Morgan said.

"Get someone on *Flint.* Get your geek intel on it and see if the victims had profiles there. Then get him to track the IP address of whoever was hacking the site for their personal information."

"Son of a bitch," said Morgan. "They hacked a dating site to laser-target the victims and find their addresses."

"It's a hunch," I said, thinking of Liz Durison's rosé-swilling ghost, and the look she had given me when I had thought about the dating app.

"It's more than a hunch," said Morgan, her excitement lifting the tone of her voice. "If you're right, we've got the mothertrucker by the ball-hairs."

I winced, thinking of the smell of Slyden's torpedoed nether regions. I didn't want to think about ball hairs, singed or not. But I did want to catch this gang of murderers.

"I'll meet you at HQ," I said, and hung up, ignoring the twenty-eight messages I had from Tambo Vuleka, the owner of the *Olde Worlde Railways.* The starry-eyed tourists would have to wait. We had a killer cult to catch.

CHAPTER 29

WINNOW

When I arrived at the Scorpions' HQ there were already three unmarked vehicles twirling their emergency lights, revving, ready to go. Agents were patting down their bullet-proof jackets, checking their guns, and jumping into the growling cars.

"You were right," said Morgan, out of breath. "They were all on *Flint*. The V-Cult killers were hacking the site, using face-mapping tech to find women who fitted the profile."

I nodded.

Morgan ripped the velcro strap on her jacket to tighten it, her red nails bright against the black fabric of the kevlar. "We're triangulating the physical address of the perp. Chuck Winnow. We're going right now, as soon as it comes through. We might even be able to save her."

Her? I thought. I didn't yet know her name. *Victim number nine. Rise and Shine.*

"I'm coming with you," I said, jumping into Morgan's SUV, forgetting the promise I made to myself to never drive with her again.

"It'll be dangerous," said Morgan, and I laughed. What else could I do, after the day I'd had?

She climbed in, too, and the doors closed and locked around us. Bulletproof. She switched on the ignition and pumped the gas, so that her car joined in, purring with the others, waiting for the address to show up on the screen. The sun began to peek out from the cityscape, tinting the buildings with light the color of marmalade.

"Come on," she said, staring at the screen in the middle of her dash. "Come on!"

"Morgan, I need a favor," I said.

She looked across at me with incredulity on her face, the flashing lights of the other cars lighting up her pale face with red, then blue, then red again.

"God knows I love you, Jax," she said. "But this isn't a great time."

"It's important," I said.

Seriously? Her face said. *Seriously?* But then she turned off the engine and faced me properly. "You have my attention."

"Can you send a squad car somewhere for me, now?"

"Now?" said Morgan. "It's four-thirty in the morning."

"We don't have time to talk about the details," I said. "But there is an evil wizard locked in his basement at 106 Merlin Drive, Orange Grove."

She blinked at me, possibly wondering if I had gone mad, or was pulling her leg, or both.

"I've already hotlined the Council," I said, "but I haven't heard back. That's really unusual, so I just want to make sure he doesn't escape to harm anyone else."

By anyone else, *I specifically meant* me. If Slyden was ever let free, my days—my *hours*—would be numbered. And Blimaex would be dead, too. I felt for the voodoo doll in my pocket, hoping that the wizard was finally out of pain, or, at the very least, out of immediate danger.

"I know it sounds crazy," I said. "But the threat is real."

Morgan looked forward again, clenching her jaw and drumming her fingers on her steering wheel. I knew why she was hesitating. She didn't have the manpower or the budget for this kind of thing. She had already borrowed resources for the dawn raid. The extra team would raise a lot of questions, and the Scorpions did not like questions. Questions got units like theirs disbanded.

"I'm going to have some explaining to do," she said, shaking her head, then picked up her transceiver and called it in.

As soon as the dispatcher noted down Slyden's details, the message came through with Chuck Winnow's address.

Morgan typed it onto her navigator screen and flicked a switch, letting her siren wail, and I was pressed back into my seat with the force of her foot on the accelerator as we sped out of the parking area and onto the highway.

The address was in Sunninghill, just a few minutes out of Sandton, where the land is developed to within an inch of its life. Security complexes racked and stacked alongside each other like trees in a forest, racing upwards for the sunshine. The resulting traffic is one reason to stay away, the concordant hijacking rate is another. As soon as the light turns red, a pack of hawkers descend on the jammed cars, offering their wares through the windows. On a good day you'll have Fong Kong shades, phone chargers and fizzy drinks held up to your temple. On a bad day it'll be a nine millimeter, and you'll be walking home. On a very bad day you won't be walking anywhere ever again.

Morgan and her entourage ploughed through the early morning queues of cars, her siren and flashing lights acting like a magical staff, parting the metal and rubber that stood in our way. As the cars peeled off around us, rubbernecking, I made sure I was ready for the confrontation. I took my arm out of the makeshift T-shirt sling—it was feeling much better—and I buttoned my trench coat right up to the collar and tightly belted it.

"What happened to your arm?" Morgan asked.

I thought of Gnor, snoring in my doorway. "You don't want to know," I replied.

"And your hand?" she asked. It was still blackened by the intense lightning spell I had slung at Slyden. I shook it out and then covered it with the sleeve of my coat.

"If we survive this," I said, "You can buy me one of those overpriced cocktails and I'll tell you everything."

Morgan checked her rearview mirror and overtook a minibus taxi that was slowing for a passenger in quite possibly the most dangerous section of the road. "Deal," she said, and accelerated again.

According to the nav screen, we'd be at our destination in two minutes. I started to feel my anxiety climb, and could smell my stale sweat.

Morgan picked up her transceiver to message the other vehicles. "Quiet approach," she said, and the cars' sirens were all switched off.

"You ready to nail these guys?" I asked.

"Born ready," she said, her eyes as fierce as I had ever seen them.

THE SQUAD CARS had pre-clearance at the complex, which was designed and decorated in a cheap knockoff of an Italian villa: low-cost South African bricks plastered and then painted to look like burnished Italian clay; straggly pines planted to conceal the myriad rubbish bins; and a concrete-molded water feature in the middle of the residents' parking area. The unmarked police cars rushed in, and some of the officers were out of the cars, guns-in-hand, before the vehicles were even stationary.

No one said a word as we ran toward Winnow's door, numbered 16. It was on the ground floor, at the end of a short path lined with dead plants. The only sound was boots hitting tarmac, and then clay floor tiles. The cars' radios crackled in the distance. Morgan gave a signal to one of her officers, the most muscle-bound among them, and he nodded. He was about to slam his shoulder up against the door, but I grabbed him just in time. Wired on adrenaline and testosterone, he looked at me as if he'd like to slam me into the door, too. I unclipped my wand and whispered: "*Fiat Fulgar.*"

A light blue stream of current flowed out of my wand and into the lock mechanism of the door, melting it quietly so as to not alert the people inside. The scent of charred wood reached us, Morgan gave the next signal, and the black uniforms pushed open the door and scuttled into the small apartment. I could smell the guns and the stress in the air, like ozone, and there was something else. Something sweet.

The entrance hall was empty, as was the kitchen (apart from a weeks' dirty dishes). The counter was strewn with old takeaway pizza boxes and polystyrene burger clamshells. Sour milk and barbecue sauce.

"He's here," I whispered to Morgan, pointing at the still-steaming kettle next to a fresh bakery box stained with frosting: strawberry, with sprinkles. Chuck Winnow was there, and he was eating freaking donuts.

THE BEDROOM and bathroom were clear, which left us with one last room, the door of which was locked. The barrel-chested man looked at me, and I raised my wand.

"Fiat Fulgur," I whispered, and the current left my body and zapped the lock. Then, the time for keeping quiet was over. Brawn kicked open the door, and the uniforms strode in like soldiers, all yelling at the same time. They waved their heavy black guns around and shouted at the man at the desk, who jumped up in shock and raised his hands.

"Don't move!"

"Chuck Winnow!"

"We have you surrounded!"

Brawn pointed his Beretta straight at Winnow's forehead and applied just enough pressure to the trigger to make Chuck want his mama.

"Move a goddamned muscle," said Brawn, "and I promise you it'll be the last thing you ever do."

Winnow raised his hands, showing off his damp underarms. The half-eaten pink donut dropped from his shaking fingers. There was the smell of urine in the closed space, and I saw the wet patch on Winnow's chinos spreading. His face was as round and white as a paper plate.

Disappointment chilled my bones as I realized then that we would not be finding victim number nine there. Or the murderers. I took Morgan's arm.

"It's not him," I said.

CHAPTER 30

MORGUE MUGSHOTS

Morgan looked at me so ferociously I'm surprised she didn't snap her neck. "What are you talking about?" she said. "Of course it's him."

"This is the correct address," said Brawn.

Morgan faced one of the smaller cops, the one without a gun, wearing black-rimmed glasses. "Check," she said, and motioned to Winnow's computer. The man took over Chuck's computer.

She turned to the man. "Are you Chuck Winnow?" she barked at him.

The man was sweating profusely. His eyes darted around the room as if looking for a way to escape.

Morgan took a step toward him and pointed her gun at his chest. "Are you Chuck Winnow?" she asked again, through gritted teeth.

"Yes," he said. "Yes." He was nodding; short, jerky movements. Morgan smiled at me. It was a hard expression that wasn't really a smile at all. The officer with the black-rimmed glasses began tapping away at the keyboard.

Winnow started stuttering something.

Morgan raised her gun again. "Speak up!"

"Sh-she told me sh-she was eighteen," he said.

"Who?" she demanded. "Where is she?"

"What do you mean?" he asked, frowning.

"The girl!" Morgan yelled. "Where is the girl?"

"I don't know!" Chuck said. "At home? In China? It was weeks ago!"

"Not the same girl," I said to Morgan, although she didn't want to hear it. *Not victim number nine. Not the murderer.*

Chuck Winnow was not the type to lead a serial killer cult as organized as the V-Cult. He didn't wash dishes, and he ate pink donuts for breakfast. He was wearing a grubby shirt that was too tight over his beer belly. His desk was strewn with stained coffee mugs—one of them sporting a *Darth Vader* mask—and toy figurines. He had wet his pants just looking up the barrel of a gun. I wanted this guy to be guilty as much as Morgan did, wanted the killings to stop, but Chuck Winnow was not our man.

The cop with the black-rimmed glasses smashed a couple more keys and then turned the computer screen to face us.

"Bingo," he said. The screen showed the back-end of the *Flint* application, and Winnow's grubby paw prints were all over it.

Morgan didn't lower her weapon. "You'd better start talking."

"*FLINT?* Is that what this is about?" asked Chuck. His relief was palpable, although his face was still stamped with confusion. One of the officers came out of Winnow's bedroom and threw him a pair of shorts. Morgan and I averted our gaze while he quickly changed out of his wet chinos.

"I can tell you anything you need to know about *Flint,*" he said. "I've been working on it for some time."

"Hacking it, you mean," said Morgan.

"Well," said Chuck, shrugging. "Yes." He ran his fingers through his hair, and I could tell that he was still shaking.

"Why?" Brawn asked.

"It started as a hobby. I found a way to manipulate the algorithms so that I could get more impressions. Then I learned I could also manipulate it the other way, to get only the right kinds of girls to respond to my profile."

"The right kind of girls?" Morgan asked.

"You know," he said, still perspiring. "My type."

"And what is that?" asked Morgan. "Tall, brunette, athletic?"

Chuck frowned again. "No," he said. "Petite. Asian."

"Go on," I said.

"So I use a combination of digital face-mapping on the profile pictures, and add the data set to that."

"Data set?"

"Profile information, you know. Height, weight, hobbies. And then it narrows the list down so that I don't waste my time on imperfect matches."

"What do you do for a living, Mr. Winnow?" Morgan asked.

"I'm an... IT consultant?" Chuck said.

"You're a hacker," she said.

"Well, yes," he said, then hastened to add, "But I don't do anything illegal."

"Ha," said Morgan. "Famous last words."

His cheeks regained some color.

"And this particular hack," said Morgan. "This targeting you do on *Flint*."

"I wouldn't call it *targeting*," he said. "That seems a bit—"

"This targeting you do," Morgan said again, as if she hadn't heard him interrupt. "You do it for other people. They pay you."

"Yes," he said. "That's not illegal." His cheeks blushed some more. "Is it?"

The cop with the glasses piped up. He had been digging deeper into Winnow's machine. "He runs a gamut of services like this one. Has a record of micropayments from all over the world."

"Let me guess," said Morgan, clenching her fist. "They're all untraceable."

"Yep," said the cop. "And the *Flint* profiles of the men Durison had contact with are all scrambled. Same with the other vics."

Morgan's cheeks flushed with fury.

"You were given a job to target woman who look like me," I said, and Chuck looked at me as if it was the first time he had seen me in the room. He blinked and chewed his lips.

He chose his words carefully. "I get lots of different jobs."

"But this one," I pushed. "This particular one. Started around a week ago. Tall. Brunette. Athletic. With a face like mine."

"I guess so," he said.

He was lying about something.

"You guess so?"

Morgan took a step closer to him to remind him of what was at stake.

"Okay," he said. "Yes. Yes, I had to find women that looked like you."

I stared at him, my stomach roiling with fear and fury. Without meaning to, angry magic flowed out of my fingers, waiting for my command. I had none. My hands sparked blue as I tried to calm down.

Chuck stared harder. "What the—"

But I couldn't hold it in anymore. I was so angry that this was happening to these women, any one of them who could have been me, that my magic was trying to jump out of my skin.

"Jax," said Morgan, when she saw my face.

I needed to get out of there, needed to decompress before I blew that stupid Italian villa apartment away, but it was like I couldn't move. My own magic was keeping me fused to the floor, insisting on retribution.

This isn't the guy, I told myself. It didn't help.

Ventum Exquiris, I heard myself think, without meaning to. Soon a wind whipped up inside the room, sending papers and old paper serviettes flying around us. Then it got harder, and mugs began crashing to the floor, toys toppled over, and everyone in the room looked shocked, including Morgan.

"Jax," she said, her eyes flashing a warning.

I looked back at her with desperate eyes. *It's not me,* I wanted to say, but it very clearly was.

The whirlwind got stronger, and we all looked for something to hold on to, or risk being flung into the amaretti-colored walls. The cops held on to their hats and their guns. Cerulean light flowed from my palms and joined the sweeping wind, till the gust was veined with blue. My arms were lifting, and they began to sway above my head, as if I was directing the wind... which I was, but I wasn't. The same thing had happened to me when I was chasing down the leader of the goblin gang the week before. Qwynkle had made me so furious that I ended up destroying an entire basement parking level and I almost killed myself in the process. I had lost control of my emotion, and thus lost control of my magic. I needed to bring myself down, but the blue kept streaming from my hands. Soon the drawers of Winnow's desk flew out and smashed into the wall opposite, and the contents went flying around the room, including a photograph of me, which Morgan expertly plucked out of the rushing air as if her hand was a hungry bird. She looked down at it, then stared at me.

"Jax!" shouted Morgan, which broke the spell, literally and figuratively, and the whirling air stopped. Everything that had been swept up in the air fell back down with a disappointed tumble, including the *Darth Vader* mug that shattered onto Chuck's desk right in front of him, making everyone jump.

Chuck's body and voice were trembling. "That was my favorite mug."

So much for us all doing our bit to preserve the Masquerade. I had just outed myself as a wizard in front of our prime suspect.

"Can someone please tell me what is g-going on?" he said. He looked at me again. "Who *are* you?"

Morgan held up the photograph. From what I could tell, it had been taken recently, just outside my apartment building. Morgan looked as spooked as I felt. "Who hired you?"

"I don't know!" Chuck said. "I never know. It's best to keep both parties anonymous."

"You're going to go to prison," said Morgan.

The color left Chuck's cheeks again. "But I haven't done anything wrong!"

Morgan, still clutching the photo of me, leaned in to him and spoke in a terrifying whisper. So terrifying that I worried for the dryness of his new shorts. "You are going to prison for aiding and abetting a serial killer."

"No!" shouted Chuck. "I didn't!"

With a roar, Morgan slid her arm over the desk and swept everything onto the floor, including the fragments of

Chuck's favorite mug. When the counter was clear, she tore open the velcro straps of her bulletproof vest and plunged her hand into her pocket underneath, bringing out a stack of small photographs: morgue mugshots.

"Liz Durison!" she shouted, slamming the first photo on the desk in front of him. His eyes grew wider, and his skin took on a green tinge. It was clear that he recognized her.

"I didn't know about this," he said.

"Stacy Morrow!" Morgan shouted, and the next photo was slammed down. Winnow's face was a mask of horror. He looked up at me, and then back at the photograph.

"No," he said. "No, no, no."

"Tammy Bachman!" yelled Morgan, and kept going until there were eight photos on the table.

"No," said Winnow again.

"Yes!" shouted Morgan. "And you're going to tell us who has been paying you to find these women!"

"I don't know!" he shouted back. "I swear, I don't know!" and then he grabbed the wastepaper basket that was at his feet and vomited into it. Again, I averted my eyes.

The half-eaten donut lay forgotten on the floor.

CHAPTER 31

CONTAGIOUS MAGIC

When Morgan dropped me off outside my apartment I was seriously on edge. Who had taken that photo of me? And who had sent it to Chuck Winnow? (Chuck Winnow, who was now being interrogated at the Scorpions' HQ by Brass Balls, AKA Captain Morgan. He didn't stand a chance). If there was something he hadn't told us, Morgan would get it out of him. In the meantime, I was under strict instructions to sleep, because I was so worn out by the time we all piled back into the squad cars that I was slurring with exhaustion. I wanted to go along to the HQ for Chuck Winnow's questioning, but I could hardly string a sentence together and remembered that I hadn't eaten much or slept for over 24 hours. A wizard has got to know her limitations. I felt awful climbing into bed without having gone to investigate the attacks at the *Olde Worlde Railway,* and worse about not going to check on Blimaex since I had locked his brother up and stolen the voodoo doll, but if I didn't get some sleep I wouldn't be of any use to anybody. You know that advice they give when they're briefing you on the safety drill on board a plane?

In the case of an emergency, first make sure your own oxygen mask is in place before you help anyone else.

Well, my whole week had been a plane crash, and I needed my bloody oxygen mask. It had felt like years since I had last been home. I greeted Gnor, my security guard, with all the enthusiasm I could muster, and practically fell into my apartment. I gulped down the last two painkillers in the bottle with a glass of much-needed tap water, then I filled the tumbler up again. I was so thirsty that I almost didn't bother with the glass. My skin had a layer of grime on it so thick you'd think I'd been sweeping chimneys all day. My shirt smelled so bad that I didn't even bother slinging it in the laundry hamper. Instead, it went straight into the bin. I could practically hear Ghost tut-tutting at my slovenly behavior. I didn't even wait for the reprimand-slash-greeting of the red hardcover slamming to the floor. I just crawled into the shower and turned it on full-blast. After one minute I felt noticeably better. After ten minutes I had scrubbed my skin, washed my hair, and the drugs had kicked in. I felt a million times better—I was pretty much high—and I started singing to prove it.

Now, if I was an ordinary human with an ordinary vocal range and rhythm, this may not have been a problem, but I am known for my shocking singing voice. *It's enough to send werewolves running,* Ferra had said once, when we had a magical karaoke evening at *The Copper Cog & Ale*. And what could I say? I agreed. So, I didn't sing. Unless I was alone, in the shower, feeling lucky to be alive, and high on painkillers that were so strong they could have flattened a troll.

I turned off the shower, still warbling, then reached for my towel, which I had forgotten to hang over the side of the shower door.

"Faex!"

Suddenly, among the cloud of steam, the offending towel appeared.

Oh my word, I thought, *is Ghost stepping up his game? Handing me towels after I shower? It's like having a butler! I could get used to this.*

"Ghost?" I asked. This was unprecedented. I began fantasizing about all the things Ghost could do for me. Blitz *Piña Coladas* for me in summer, brew spicy *Gluhwein* in winter. Would he now start answering the door and ironing my newspapers?

"Ghost?"

I wrapped the towel around myself and climbed out of the goblin-sized shower. The golden light of the sunrise was streaming into the bedroom, gilding the man in the chair.

Darick looked up at me and grinned. "I've been called worse," he said.

I blushed. Not because I was half naked, but because he had been subjected to my singing. Is that why he was grinning like a lunatic? Probably.

I knew that I should have said:

Darick, you can't just keep showing up like this. I was in the shower.

I am half naked, for faex's *sake.*

You can't come and go as you please.

This is my personal space.

I am going to fire Gnor.

You need to phone ahead, you need to knock on the door, you need to ask if you can come in.

But I knew that I meant none of it. I loved that Darick had the habit of showing up exactly when I needed him. And this *personal space* had been too lonely and cold for too long. We stood there, not saying a word, and it was as if we understood each other. In a strange way, we had always understood each other. I took a few steps toward him.

Darick looked at the charm bracelet on my dripping wrist, the one he had given me, with the exploded goblin bullet as its only charm. The one he had dug out of my heart before using his power to heal me.

Darick. Mage. Assassin.

He stopped smiling. There was something else on his face, now.

"You still wear it," he said, his voice gruff.

"I've never taken it off," I said.

He stood up, out of the chair he had spent whole nights awake in, watching me sleep, guarding over me. He moved toward me, his huge chest rising and falling, the bronze honey light streaming over both of us. And then we were standing together, almost touching, looking into each other's eyes. *Almost touching.* My body was humming with my longing for him, and his face reflected my desire. He reached for my face, laid his palm gently on the side of my head. He glanced at the tattoo on my neck—a vampire bite — and with his other hand he pulled me closer, a quick, decisive gesture that thrilled me, and I let the towel drop onto the floor. His eyes were on fire, then, as was my skin where he touched me. I needed more. I wanted every inch of him. I reached up and our lips were a whisper away from touching when my phone began to ring.

CHAPTER 32

CRUEL CARVINGS

Darick picked my towel up off the floor and handed it to me. I quickly wrapped it around my aching body and checked my phone, which I hated with all my being at that exact moment. The caller ID flashed *SCORPIONS* so I didn't have a choice but to answer it. Darick left the room, closing the door to give me some privacy.

"Morgan?"

"Jax. You're supposed to be sleeping."

"So you decided to phone and wake me up to check?"

"I have to tell you something."

"I'm listening hard," I said.

"The address you gave us. Orange Grove? We sent a squad car to pick the guy up. There was no one there."

My body went cold.

"In the basement," I said. "I locked him in the basement."

"I know. They checked. The trapdoor was open. All they found down there was an empty cage."

"No!" I shouted into the phone, and kicked the wall, almost breaking my toes.

"I'm really sorry," she said.

"He had help," I said. "Someone helped him escape."

"Who?"

I shook my head. "I don't know."

"It's been a tough day. And it's only six a.m."

If Slyden was free, it would probably be my last day alive. I slumped onto my bed.

"It could improve," said Morgan.

"Somehow I don't think that's going to happen."

"There is some good news," she said.

"What?"

"I got a court order to suspend *Flint's* services. Temporarily."

"That is good news," I said. "Well done."

"The judge gave us 48 hours."

"*Filius Canis,*" I muttered.

"It's something."

I put Morgan on speakerphone and began to pull on my clothes.

"What are you doing?" she asked.

"Getting dressed."

"No," she said. "You're supposed to be sleeping."

"So you keep saying," I said, wrenching my tight jeans up and hopping on the spot to speed up the process.

"Now? Morning aerobics?" asked Morgan.

"Skinny jeans," I said.

"Ah."

The doorbell rang.

"Argh," I said. "The door. I've gotta go. I'll call you."

"Can I help?" she said. "With the missing wizard?"

I felt cold at the mention of him. He would be on his way to find me, and this time he wouldn't give me the chance to escape. I needed all the help I could get, but there was no way I'd drag Morgan into this. It was way too dangerous.

I OPENED the door to a hopeful Bron. He smiled and held up a takeaway coffee for me.

"Ah, *faex*," I said when I saw him, and his face dropped. "Sorry, Bron, I completely forgot about our session today."

I took the coffee anyway, and had a gulp. It was exactly what I needed. "May the Void bless you," I said.

Honestly, I was a little surprised he showed up. He had seemed really spooked after our last training session, and I had wondered if he would decide that the magical life was not for him after all. Gnor snored alongside us, practically supine in the brittle plastic garden chair.

"I've been practicing," Bron said, the jade buttons of his eyes bright against his dark skin.

"Good," I said. "Good."

"I won't get scared again," he said.

"Believe me, you'll get scared," I told him. "The trick is to not let the fear rule you."

"I'll get better, I promise," he said. "I've been practicing, non-stop. I want to show you."

He stood there, watching me, still hopeful.

"I need to be somewhere this morning," I said to him. "Sorry. We'll continue your lessons tomorrow."

If I'm still breathing, I thought.

"I could just follow you around today," he said. "I won't say anything. I'll just watch."

"No," I said. "Not today."

"I'll just shadow you," he said.

"Bron," I said, my eyes drilling into his. "Not today. Okay?"

The boy was really disappointed. He didn't even say good-bye. He just narrowed his eyes and with a loud snapping sound he turned into a raven and flew away.

"Thank you for the coffee!" I yelled after him.

Gnor woke with a start. "What that?"

"Never mind, Gnor," I said. "Go back to sleep."

DARICK WAS in the kitchen when I traipsed back inside. He was examining the plant, which had doubled in size, and was now covering most of the window.

"That crown is somewhere," he said. "Somewhere close."

He broke a small piece of the plant off and put it in his jacket pocket.

"Gizmo might be alive, too," I said, hope cracking my voice.

"Yes," Darick said, although the word sounded empty to my ears.

I HAD TO GO. I would have said *Make yourself at home*, but Darick had done that a long time ago.

I gave him what was left of my coffee and pulled my trench coat on.

"I have an assignment," I told him, even though he didn't ask. My coat felt heavy, which is when I remembered all the things I had in my infinity pocket. I pulled out Durison's little black book, and Zeel's notebook, and squeezed them into my already bursting bookshelf, in-between *Fantastical Fae Folklore* and *The ShadowChaser*. While Darick's back was turned, I took the small brown bottle of *Spiritus Morbus* and hid it behind the top row of books. Then I took out the voodoo doll of Blimaex Abarim and laid it gently on the kitchen counter. It still had the Latin fairytale carved into its body.

"What is it?" Darick asked.

"It's a poppet someone was using to transmit Contagious Magic," I said. "A voodoo doll."

Darick leaned in closer, looking at the engraving. "That must've hurt."

"Can you fix it?" I asked.

"Heal it?" he said. "A doll?"

"It's still linked to the recipient," I said. "I don't know how to break the connection."

Darick looked thoughtful, then he rubbed his palms together, as if warming them up.

"I don't know if it'll work," he said. "But I can try."

He kept rubbing his hands together until they seemed to emit a subtle glow, which I hadn't seen before. Perhaps the glow had been inside my body when he had sewn me up. He gazed at the wooden figurine in deep concentration, then laid his right hand on it, covering it from head to toe. His chest rose and fell as he breathed deeply, not taking his eyes off his glowing hand. When he had finished, and raised it again, the voodoo doll had a smooth, polished exterior, without a trace of the previous cruel carvings.

"Thank you," I said. "Thank you."

I put the doll back in my pocket. I'd give it to Blimaex. He'd know what to do with it.

MY PHONE RANG WITHIN MINUTES. It was Willard, the butler. His voice wobbled with relief.

"I don't know what you did," he said, "I don't know how you did it."

"He's better?"

"Ms. Knight," Willard said. "He's better. He was dying. He was close to the end. But now he's better." And then he broke down in tears.

I looked over at Darick and smiled at him. "It worked," I whispered away from the phone, and he smiled back.

I turned my attention back to Willard. "I'm on my way to you," I said. "I have something for Blimaex."

"Thank you," he said, through muffled sobs.

"I just have a quick stop to make, first."

"Thank you," he said again.

"Willard?" I said. "I think I may have upset Slyden."

Willard stopped gushing; his joy evaporated.

"What?"

"I'll be there as soon as I can. But in the meantime... lock the doors."

MY TRENCH COAT was belted tightly. I had my wand clipped to my belt, and my brand new crossbow on my back. Darick blinked at me.

"Going shopping?" he joked.

Yep, I thought. *I'm going shopping for vampires.*

There was no way I was going to hang around at home waiting for Slyden to find me and my snoring security guard, and I was way overdue at *The Olde Worlde Railway.*

My plan was to head over to the railway station, ash the few vampires that were causing trouble for the owner, then go to Abarim Manor to hand over the voodoo doll.

I'm not going to even try to look for Slyden, I thought, my stomach doing a tumble-turn. I knew that he would find me.

CHAPTER 33

A LITTLE VAMPIRE PROBLEM

Darick picked up his keys and looked ready to go. He didn't ask me where I was going.

"I'll walk you out," he said, looking at his watch. "I have to be somewhere."

Part of me wanted him to come with me and help sort out the couple of troublemakers at the railway station. Another part of me reminded myself that I did this for a living. I pictured my bedpost in my head. I didn't need a man by my side to take care of a little vampire problem.

I couldn't help it, though. I felt a little put out that he wasn't coming with me. Assignment or not, I understood with a fluttering feeling in my stomach that I wanted to spend more time with Darick. The threat of Slyden hanging over me like a thudding storm cloud added to my inclination to hang on to him. I admit, it's pretty handy to have a healing mage-slash-assassin around.

We said goodbye at my motorbike, and almost kissed again. His hand was electric on my back. I slammed my helmet on and revved my bike and we waved as I zoomed out of the building's parking lot.

THE RIDE to the *Olde Worlde Railway* station was heady and filled with mixed emotions. My mind and body were still buzzing from having Darick in my bedroom, and my skin was tingling all over. It's a unique kind of thrill when you understand that someone you have been falling for is falling along with you. I couldn't let my guard down though, I reminded myself. The stark truth was that I still had no idea who Darick was or what he was doing in my life. His name still had a vampiric ring to it, I thought, but he was no vampire. Or if he was, he was hiding it extremely well.

In fact, I had a feeling he was hiding a lot, and was very good at doing so. I made up my mind, then, as I rode past the Ponte Tower—a vast cylindrical structure in hacked gray concrete, 54 stories high, notorious for its New Brutalism architecture and suicidal occupants—that I was going to find out who Darick was before falling any harder.

The image of the tower stayed in my head. I had read somewhere that when it fell into disrepair, the people tossed their garbage down its hollow core, and when the rubbish was finally cleared, there were three stories of it, and it included, amongst other horrifying things, dead bodies of animals and humans. I hoped that I wouldn't come to regret digging into Darick's past.

. . .

I ARRIVED at the railway station, my bike's tires skidding slightly on the loose gravel in the parking lot. The place looked deserted, and I wondered if Tambo Vuleka had, after all, managed to get the tourists to stop coming in. I walked, tentatively, over the sharp gray stones, toward the reception, which looked like an 1800s railway station, replete with a grand building painted a handsome navy blue, a beautiful steam locomotive on the tracks, and the smell of burning coal in the air.

"Hello?" I called. "Mister Vuleka?"

The place remained silent, and empty.

This isn't creepy at all, I thought to myself. *Nope, not creepy.*

I touched the crossbow on my back, just to reassure myself. There would be vampires there, and I would ash them. Nothing to get nervous about. Still, I felt adrenaline start to push through my veins, lighting me up from the inside. It was as if my body could feel the evil in the air and was reacting accordingly. All I could do was keep walking.

I arrived on the platform, which was as neat as a pin, and totally empty. The shiny maroon train on the track before me hissed, and a plume of white smoke swirled out of it, into the fresh morning sky. It seemed ready to go somewhere, but Vuleka had said that he had shut the whole operation down. Had he changed his mind? Had the vampires moved on to other vintage tourist destinations? I kept moving forward.

The reception desk looked abandoned. I leaned over the counter to see if I could catch a glimpse of anyone behind the scenes when a man popped out from behind a store-room door, making me jump a foot in the air.

"Ms. Knight!" he practically yelled. "Thank you for coming!"

I would have replied, but I was trying to convince my lungs to start breathing again, and my heart not to go into cardiac arrest.

Vuleka was dressed as the conductor in a smart old-school suit with color-coded epaulets and bow-tie, and peaked hat. The gold chain of his pocket watch glinted as he moved.

"Sorry!" he said, "Sorry! I can see I startled you. That was not my intention."

You were just so happy to see me, I thought.

"I am just so happy to see you!" he gushed. Something about his words sounded odd. Rehearsed. Maybe I was just being paranoid. Maybe there was nothing suspicious about him, apart from the fact that he clearly watched too many wooden-dialogue films.

Again, I wasn't in the mood for small talk. "Where are they?"

The conductor looked at me, took in my wand, and the crossbow clipped to my back.

"That's all you have?" he asked.

"It's all I need," I said.

"Please," he motioned to the train. "Come this way."

The train hissed again as the man strode toward it. Vuleka hopped on board and offered his hand.

"You want me to get on the train?" I asked.

My gut instinct was saying *Hellz No.*

Fighting vampires was one thing, but fighting vampires on a moving train with nowhere to run? That didn't seem like the best way to keep oneself alive.

"Well," he said, blinking. "They're on the train."

Those bad films he'd been watching: Snakes on a Plane? I wondered. No, then he'd know there's no way any sensible person would agree to *Vampires on a Train.*

I took a step back from the carriage. I admit that I make a lot of mistakes, but I don't often ignore my gut instinct. And my instinct was yelling at me to sprint, screaming, in the opposite direction. I took another step backwards. I could be on my bike in less than ten seconds.

Every part of my body was shouting *Run! Run! Run!*

"I'm sorry," I said. "I don't think I can help you, after all."

Vuleka blinked at me, clutching the elegant silver whistle that hung around his neck.

It wasn't fear that was driving me back... was it? I had faced my fears over and over again since I had taken up arms against the creatures who had killed my parents. But facing your fears was one thing, being reckless with your life was another. On a good day I think of myself as brave, but I'm not stupid. And today I wanted to live. I wanted to be able to see Morgan again, and Ferra. I wanted to spend time with Darick, whether he was hiding something or not.

I took another step backwards. I was going to run for it. I was about to apologize for the last time when my body bumped up against something. Startled, I spun around, grabbing my wand as I did so, and saw... the conductor. I looked back at the conductor on the train, who was now expressionless, then at the one I had just bumped into, who also wore Vuleka's face, and Vuleka's uniform, like an identical twin. Then I saw movement on the platform; in the distance, another three conductors were marching toward us. All five of the identical men's eyes were trained on me, hawk-like.

My mind was spinning; I couldn't make sense of what was happening, but I felt the menace like glinting daggers in the air. My crossbow thrummed on my back, my wand buzzed in my hand. I had a lot to live for. If they wanted a fight, they'd get one.

I COULD HANDLE FIGHTING five men, I thought, and I steadied my stance. The conductor right next to me, who I had bumped into, made a grab for my wand, but I moved it away from him just in time, across my chest, then swung my elbow back in his direction, catching him in the throat. He lurched back, and his hands flew up to his neck as he choked.

"Ignem Exquiris!" My spell burnt though my body and through my arm, and the current that left my wand was a searing blue bolt of lightning that took the man out at the knees. He fell over and shouted in pain. The other three were closer now, almost close enough for me to deal with.

"Glaciem Exquiris!" I shouted, and my hot wand turned cold. It drew all the fear I was holding in my chest and turned it into frozen water, sending up a wall of ice between us. But I didn't have time to celebrate. There were another dozen conductor clones heading my way, and they were just as scarily expressionless as the others had been, as if they were all wearing super-realistic masks.

"Monstras!" I shouted, and a purple swirl of magic swept around me and then cascaded over to them. One by one, my reveal spell stripped away their glamours, and I saw that the men striding toward me were vampires. That's when I realized it was a trap.

CHAPTER 34

BLOOD-SCENTED VOICE

There were over a dozen teal-caped vampires striding toward me as if they hadn't eaten in days and I was a nice roast dinner with all the trimmings. Before, their glamours had been bland, but now their real faces showed all the emotions they felt. Their expressions flickered in turn with anger, satisfaction, ambition, greed, and desire.

I quickly clipped my wand back onto my belt and reached for my crossbow, which was vibrating with potential energy. It was as if the bow wanted to kill the vampires as much as I did. I took aim at the vampire in the middle of the advancing crowd and pulled the trigger. The arrow shot out of the bow with a satisfying *thwack* and sheared the air between us, stabbing my target in the heart. He shouted in pain and fury, his hands grasping the terminal shaft of the heat-seeking arrow. His nose began to bleed, then his eyes, as he sank down to the ground. None of his kin stopped to help him.

They had cold hearts, and they knew there was no saving him. Then there was a burst of light, as if a fire-breather had arrived at the party, as the wounded vampire burst into flames. He screamed as the fire licked his face, and then there was another explosion, and he was turned into sour smoke, and his body littered the platform with ash.

I aimed the crossbow and pulled the trigger again and again, and managed to pick off another five vampires who all combusted in their own way. Some of the flames were green, some purple. I didn't have time to admire the fireworks. Another wave of conductors appeared, streaming out of the station, and I knew I had no option but to jump on the steam train behind me. It was the only way I could escape them, but only if I could get it to move.

I swapped my crossbow for my wand and yelled *"Contendis!"* but the train was extremely heavy, and it looked like my magic alone wouldn't move it.

"Contendis!" I shouted again. The train inched forward and stopped.

The vampires were too close. Close enough to swoop and grab me. I wasn't going to let that happen. *"Contendis! Contendis!"*

The train limped forward, and then the vampires were right outside, ready to jump aboard. I ashed the vampire closest to me, then pointed my wand inside the train, at the cab in the front carriage, and focused on the sliding door that separated us.

"Rumpis!" I yelled, and a comet of destructive yellow energy moved through my arm and blasted the door open, revealing the stoker's firebox. The flames were low.

I kept my wand stretched out toward the front cab and stared at the box. *"Ignem Exquiris!"* I shouted, and the fire erupted into a roaring blaze. Sparks and cinders burst into the carriage. With a slow, heavy chugging sound the train finally began to move.

The vampires looked worried—a prowl of hungry cats that were in danger of losing their canary—and began to climb onto the moving carriage.

"Fiat Fulgur!" I yelled, blasting the beautiful unique door of the carriage away, along with one of the vamps. Then I repeated the spell at the window, wrecking that, too, as well as a particularly ugly vampire who was trying to squeeze through. They were shouting, running next to the train, ready to fling themselves in, but the engine went faster and faster until they could no longer keep up, and soon the *Olde Worlde Railway* station was a speck in the distance.

I checked for any rogue vamps that may have been hanging on, but the carriage was clear. I clipped my wand to my belt with a sigh of relief, and bent down, hands on knees, to catch my breath.

"Holy *Faex,*" I said out loud. *That was close.*

The fire was still blazing away in the firebox, and the train was picking up speed. The pressure gauges were all red-lining, and the steam whistle was shrieking to the sky.

THE DASHBOARD in the front cab of the steam train was screaming bloody murder. I'd have to damper the furnace in the firebox if I didn't want the train to career into something large and unmoving, like the stone mountain which I knew was at the end of the railway track.

There used to be a tunnel running through the rocky ridge, but a few years ago the roof of the underpass collapsed. Now the train glides to a stop at the foot of the mountain, the passengers disembark for an old-fashioned picnic on the wild grass next to the rock face, then head back to the Jo'burg station.

Well, the plan was for the train to stop, but I didn't know the first thing about operating an 1800s steam train. I walked unsteadily to the front cab and looked at the various vintage dials and dancing needles. They reminded me of Ferra's steampunk pub for magical creatures. I needed to choke the fire, right? How difficult could that be? I moved a few levers and pulled a yellow knob, but nothing happened. The roaring fire was burning my cheeks as I tried to figure it out. I could use a *Ventum* spell to try to blow the fire out, but it ran the risk of feeding the fire, instead, like a giant bellows, and I didn't want to make this train go any faster. Already the scenery outside was a blur. I may not know anything about trains, but I knew that this antique one was not made to go this fast.

My body was overheated, and nervous. I was sweating like a plump pig at a summer bacon festival. The heat started to make me dizzy, and I had to step back into the cooler carriage to get a grip. I could try to freeze the fire, but that didn't seem like a great idea, either. Manipulating with two extremes may have unintended consequences, like stopping the train too fast, resulting in a certain wizard being thrown through the front window.

Think, I told myself. *Think!*

(Although, in my experience, telling yourself to think often has the opposite effect, like telling someone who is freaking out not to panic).

Don't panic.

The brass-framed countdown clock was whirring away. I could imagine that it usually ticked at a lovely leisurely pace, showing the passengers how long it would take to reach the end of the track, but now it was racing, as if we were traveling so fast that we were flying through time itself. Eighteen minutes to go, it said. Seventeen. Sixteen.

I was trying to figure out what to do when I caught the faintest whiff of vampire. I spun around, but the carriage was empty.

I PULLED my trench coat tightly around myself.

"Nano. Collar," I said, and my nano jumped out of my top pocket and fastened itself around my neck. I reached for my crossbow. It was almost out of arrows, but it would still come in handy. I started walking toward the second coach, my eyes wide and focused, my nose sniffing the air. I had definitely caught the scent a minute before. I knew he was there. All I had to do was find him.

As I walked, I wondered who had set this trap. I had been under the impression that the Silvano Clan had wanted me alive, because, according to Blondie, I was the only one who knew how to find The HighFire Crown.

Then a shadow of foreboding crossed my body. If they were trying to kill me, it could only mean one thing. They had found the Crown.

I didn't want to be right about that. I really hoped I was wrong. Because if Acheron Baldassare, the head of the Silvano Clan, got his grubby hands on that crown, he'd have what he needed to turn the Realm upside down. He already had more power than any vampire had any right to, but the power of the Crown would extrapolate it in a way I didn't even want to think about. He'd have free rein in the untouched world, too, and the Masquerade would fall. The Council is the most powerful committee in the Realm, but they wouldn't be able to touch Baldassare if he was able to rebuild and stabilize his pocket realm and rule from there. This assumption of mine had Bad News written all over it, and I really hoped it wasn't true.

Maybe the Silvanos were just sick of having me around, I thought. Maybe they'd had enough of a *Girl Wizard* adding notches to her bedpost. Maybe they knew what I knew: that deep down, I had a roaring vortex of darkness that I would eventually unleash on them.

I caught the scent again, the copper crimson, and slowed my pace. I was in the third coach now, and the train was still speeding along the track as if it were a Japanese bullet train instead of a locomotive. I guess even trains have their ambitions.

I SAW A FOOT. It extended past the seat, into the aisle, in the second half of the carriage. The sock was black and beige, diamond-patterned, and the shoe was a shiny leather lace-up. Conductor shoes. I clutched my crossbow tightly and inched forward. It didn't look like the foot of someone who was about to leap up and sink their fangs into my neck. It looked decidedly flaccid, as if the owner was taking a nap. Without making a sound, I crept closer, and closer. The foot didn't move. Eventually, hardly breathing, fingers perspiring on the bow, I was able to glimpse the body, and I really wish I hadn't.

It was Vuleka—the real Vuleka—dressed in his smart conductor's uniform, which had been shredded. His throat had been savagely torn open, and his bow-tie and elegant white shirt were stained with blood; in some parts bright red, and other parts, brown. His murder didn't happen here on the train, I thought. There was no blood splatter on the finely wallpapered interior. He was most likely killed at the station, and his body brought here for me to see.

A warning, or a promise.

For some reason the picture of the gypsy woman at the magical night market came into my head. The Chiromancer. She had received such a shock when she had tried to read my palm, it had thrown her and her tarot cards into the air. I wondered, then, what she had seen. My death? Or something I had to do to stay alive? Either way, things weren't looking good for me.

As if to emphasize the thought, there was a soft shuffling sound behind me, and a blood-scented voice.

It was Lysander, wiping the blood off his chin with his dark sleeve. "Jacquelyn Denna Knight," the blond vampire said, cheekbones as sharp as ever. "We meet again."

CHAPTER 35

CAT & MOUSE

"I thought you wanted me alive," I said to Lysander, trying not to look at the slick blood that still stained his face.

"Did you?" he said, amusement in his eyes. "I don't know why you'd think that. You're a vampire slayer, after all. And I'm... well, a vampire."

I glanced down at the train conductor's destroyed body, leaking onto the seat.

"Don't play games," I said.

"But games are so much fun."

"Is that why you helped me escape from the market? To play cat-and-mouse?"

He combed his fringe with his bloody fingers, transferring red highlights to his flaxen hair. "I helped you because I like you, Jacquelyn Denna Knight."

"You disgust me," I said. If I had had enough saliva in my mouth to spit at him I would have done so, but my mouth was so hot and dry it deserved its own mirage.

"I've liked you from the beginning."

"The beginning?" I laughed. "What? Yesterday?"

Lysander smiled. "No. Not yesterday."

He let that sink in, watching me squirm.

I swallowed hard. "You've been following me."

"You could say that."

I remembered, with a shudder, the picture of him standing in my kitchen, taking a photo of my pot-plant-turned-pervasive-jungle-creeper. My insides were painted with lead.

"You've found the Crown," I said, and his lips turned up at the edges. I would never get that file from him now.

"So shrewd," Lysander said. "But I knew that already."

"Give me the file," I said, not enjoying the edge of desperation I could hear in my plea. "Please."

"Why?" he said, taking the phone out of his pocket. "Why should I?"

I hated it, but I couldn't hide my vulnerability from him. I clasped my hands together and beseeched him. "Please!"

"I'm getting a feeling this is a bit of a one-way relationship," he said. "You expect me to help you, but you offer nothing in return."

"What do you want?" I asked. I was ready to say: *I'll do anything,* but the words stuck in my throat.

He looked at me, answer at the ready, when he changed his mind and shook his head.

"It's too late," he said, putting the phone away. "You had your chance."

The scenery flashed green and blue behind him. We were still going at about a brazillion miles an hour. I needed to get back to the front of the train.

I LIFTED my crossbow at him. My fingers were trembling. He looked puzzled as I aimed it at his chest.

"Why do you look puzzled, Lysander?" I asked. "After all, as you said... you're a vampire, and I'm a vampire slayer."

I saw the muscles in his jaw ripple.

I kept my grip steady. "If you're not going to give me that phone, then I'm going to have to take it from you."

Lysander narrowed his eyes at me, ready to hiss.

"It looks like today is all about last chances, Lysander, and now it's yours."

I held open my left hand, ready to receive the phone.

Lysander put his fingers to his scarlet lips. "Here's the thing," he said. "There are another fifty vampires on board, in the last few carriages."

"You're lying," I said.

"No."

"I would have seen them get on."

"No," Lysander said. "They were already on board before you arrived at the station. The vampires on the platform were just the... welcoming committee."

"To get me on the train," I said, feeling the floor vibrate violently beneath me and my heart follow chase. "Why?" I said. "Tell me the truth."

"Did you wonder at all," asked Lysander, "why I helped you to get to Slyden Abarim's house?"

Hearing the vampire say Slyden's name out loud shocked me. "What?" I said.

Maybe not quite so shrewd, after all, I heard him think. *But, still. Sexy as hell.*

My thoughts were in disarray, trying to puzzle the pieces together.

When I had arrived at Slyden's house after midnight, he had been expecting me. The wizard had set up the apparition trick and just waited for me to stumble into it. There was no way he could have known I was on my way unless someone had tipped him off. I looked at Lysander's handsome face, the drying blood on his skin turning from scarlet to brown.

When Morgan told me that Slyden had escaped the locked basement, I knew someone had helped him. I just hadn't known who. But now it made sense.

"You told Slyden that I was coming for him," I said. "And you helped him escape from the basement."

"Well," he said. "Not personally. I sent a team. But, yes. We have a longstanding agreement with Slyden Abarim."

"You offer him protection—"

"Yes."

"And he gives you his blood," I said, the idea making me feel sick. I remembered the medical fang on Slyden's desk in his sorcery chamber; the plastic tubing and the cooler box.

Magus—wizard blood—is the most potent blood on the black magic market. It's rare, for obvious reasons, and very expensive. I already knew that the Silvano Clan were collecting Magus. I had found the unmarked graves of a dozen drained and murdered wizards last week at the Obsidian Hill Cemetery.

The Silvano Clan had Magus, and they had The HighFire Crown.

The situation seemed beyond hopeless. I didn't want to live in a Realm ruled by reckless vampires. Maybe I shouldn't try to stop the train. Maybe I should let it smash into the rock face and blow us all to smithereens. It wouldn't help, though, not really, because Acheron was holed up safely in the pocket realm he was building, and he'd do it with or without us.

"Give me the phone!" I shouted. "This is the last time I'm asking."

Lysander's nostrils flared. He was not going to hand over the goods. I increased the pressure of my finger on the trigger of my crossbow, ready to send an arrow his way.

"You wouldn't," he said. Then he narrowed his eyes and I heard him think: *Would you?*

To answer his question, I pulled the trigger.

CHAPTER 36

GOLDEN AND ROSE WITH FLAME

Three things happened at once. Four, if you include my screaming.

THE ARROW LEFT the sleek flightpath of the crossbow in my hands and bolted toward Lysander's chest. The conductor sat up, ram-rod straight, and looked at me with his dead eyes. He didn't seem to care that he had neither a windpipe nor a beating heart. And a host of vampires swarmed down the train carriages, entering our coach in bloodthirsty droves.

I screamed. Of course I screamed.

Lysander's arm moved so swiftly it blurred like the outside scenery behind him. He caught my arrow just before it penetrated his breastbone, then looked at me with melty eyes, as if I had hurt his feelings by trying to rush an arrow through his heart.

I guessed an apology was in order if I wanted to survive the next sixty seconds, but as I opened my mouth, one of the other vampires was at my neck. He hissed, showing me his rabid dirty fangs, then prepared to sink them into me. I was wearing my protective nano collar, but I recoiled, regardless.

"Get off her!" shouted Lysander, confusing both the attacker and me.

The conductor, still a corpse, stood up from the soaked seat and started walking toward me. Another pair of vampires approached, looking hungry, and Lysander hissed at them. "Stay back!" he said.

Lysander had the same voracious look in his eyes, and I couldn't figure out if he was protecting me, or if he just wanted my fresh arteries for himself. He pushed the other vampires away and grabbed my arm, his fingers digging into my flesh.

He pulled me closer and whispered in my ear. "We have to get out of here."

I didn't have a choice but to follow his lead. My arm had already been ripped from its socket once in the past 24 hours, and I was out of the troll-strength painkillers. Also, there were fifty ferocious vampires clamoring for my blood, plus a conductor who hadn't yet figured out he was dead. I reckoned my chances of survival were slightly better with the turkey-carver.

"Jacqueline!" He pulled my arm again, and this time I didn't resist.

"We need to stop the train," I said. Lysander didn't answer me as we ran in the direction of the front cab. The blood-suckers followed us.

There were plenty of windows, and a few doors, which of course tempted me to jump off the locomotive. But it was speeding along the track so fast that I was sure I'd kill myself in the process. Still, if worse came to worst, I'd jump. No way I'd be a victim of one of these foul leeches. I'd take a broken neck over being a vampire's dinner every day of the week and twice on Sundays.

We kept marching toward the front of the train. What did Lysander have planned for me? I guessed I'd have to wait and see. I could hear the screaming pressure gauge before it came into view. I thought of trying an *Impedio* spell to stop the motion of the train, but the amount of energy it would require was probably more than I had to give. Or I could try *Mortales* magic: a conjuring spell. I could conjure a fire extinguisher and put out the fire in the firebox. Lysander kicked open the final door, and the scene was much worse than I had imagined. Forget about the furnace in the firebox, the whole of the front of the train was on fire.

Sometimes, when you sling a spell, the transfer of energy doesn't end there. If you are still somehow attached to the object, or the outcome, it can continue drawing energy from you. I had panicked on the platform and cast a fire spell to bolster the flames in order to get the steam train moving. It had worked really well, but I had neglected to cut off my power after the flame of the spell had taken.

Then I had caught the scent of the vampire and become distracted, as they had planned, which meant that all the fear I had felt during my grim discovery of Vuleka's body, and my confrontation with Lysander and the others, continued to feed the fire. I had expected to go back to the front cab and extinguish the fire, find the throttle or tamp the brakes to slow down the steam engine, but none of that was going to happen. The whole carriage blazed with a roaring fire; the metal turned golden and rose with flame. The heat was scorching, and Lysander and I held our arms up to our faces to protect them from the blast of fiery air. We both gasped as the heat slammed against us, burning our skin and our lungs, and we had to retreat. Still holding my arm, he searched my eyes.

Face the fifty advancing vampires with only a couple of arrows left in my bow, I thought, or face the fire? I'll be honest, neither option made my heart jump for joy. And then a third option presented itself, in a shower of sparks and glory, which happened to be the worst of the lot.

FINAL DESTINATION

As Lysander and I were watching the horror of the fire consuming the train, he loosened his fierce grip on me. His fingers traveled down my arm, and he held my hand instead. Behind us, I felt the vampires encroach. At first they entered our coach one by one, and then suddenly there were dozens: hungry eyes and bared fangs. Lysander may have been able to bat off a couple of my attackers before, but it seemed that the mob wanted what they wanted, and a sleek-cheekboned vampire wasn't going to stand in their way. The heat forced us to retreat further toward the baying crowd. Then trouble arrived.

Through the dancing flames walked a tall wizard, dressed in a hooded black robe. The fire didn't seem to bother him, and it refused to leap onto his clothes. Just clear of the blazing cab, he removed his hood and looked at me. His chalky skin and black eyes filled me with a deep, icy dread that, despite the heat of the fire, chilled the marrow of my bones. He held his staff like a weapon in his hand.

"Slyden," I said.

He looked at me with evil contempt, as if he was outraged that I had dared to cross his path again, despite the fact that he had portaled here, probably by using something I left behind in his basement. Hair, skin, blood. He stretched his arm, knotted with swollen veins, pointing his staff in my direction, and mumbled something under his breath. I let go of Lysander's hand and dove behind a seat just in time to avoid being incinerated by the bolt of electricity that had my name on it. The seat exploded backwards, hitting me as it did so. I lost my balance and tucked and rolled on the vibrating floor. I recovered quickly, jumped up into my parkour squat, and dodged another powerful blue bolt that came my way.

Lysander kept his distance from the dark wizard, and the vampires behind us stopped in their tracks, not wanting to get hit by Slyden's lightning. But they needn't have worried, because I saw the damage the last two currents had done to the wizard's hand. His papery skin was seared and blistered, and I doubted he had another bolt in him.

Slyden Abarim was more powerful than any wizard I had ever met, but he was also old, and contaminated by the Dark Arts. My guess was that he had used a considerable amount of energy to portal onto the speeding train, and would have to conserve his magic now. But just because he couldn't fling another current at me, didn't make him any less dangerous. He stepped toward me and uttered the first words I had heard him say.

"Give me the carving."

At first I was confused, and then I remembered the voodoo doll in my pocket. My stomach cramped as I realized that if we crashed into the mountain, the doll would be incinerated too, which meant that Blimaex would die along with us.

"No," I said. I was getting sick and bloody tired of being bullied for magical objects. First the crown, now the doll. Well, I'd had enough. I jumped up and pointed my wand at him. His staff may be out of juice, but my wand wasn't.

"*Glaciem Exquiris!*" I shouted, and a javelin of ice sailed through the air toward him.

"*Clipeum Glaciei!*" he said, sending up an ice-shield between us, which the javelin smashed into and splintered like broken glass.

"*Ignem Exquiris!*" I yelled, and my emotions blasted out of my wand in the form of a huge fireball, melting the shield. I quickly followed up with a bolt of electricity. "*Fiat Fulgur!*"

Bright blue lightning cracked out of my wand, toward Slyden. Without hesitation, the wizard used his staff to smack the spell back in my direction. "*Effectus Adversum!*"

I ducked behind a quaint glass divider, but not before my own spell electrocuted me in the shoulder. I felt like I had just touched an electric fence. I saw white, and my body was thrown backwards. A wave of full-body pain struck me, and my whole being felt hot and burnt inside as I hit the floor. My silver wand rolled away from me. It ended up at Lysander's feet, who I saw covertly scooping it up and putting it in his pocket.

I was on the floor, not taking my eyes off Slyden's black-veined face. I scrambled backwards, then reached for my crossbow and pointed it at the wizard, who was advancing on me, ready to finish me off. He loomed above me, seemingly ten feet high. The heat rushing from the front of the train was becoming unbearable and the scenery outside kept whizzing by. We had minutes, at the most, to stop the train or die trying.

I pulled the trigger, and the crossbow fired the third-last arrow at Slyden. *"Protendo,"* he said, swatting it away like an annoying mosquito. I dropped the crossbow, and it clattered on the floor beside me. Slyden may have been old and running low on power, but he was still the stronger wizard by miles, and he wanted me dead. He raised his staff and muttered under his breath.

"Evoco et excito, nunc et semper, res ac mortales: Sericum uitta! Ventum, Ventum, Ventum Exquiris."

A black silk ribbon slithered out of his staff and into the air above us. Then a whirlwind swept it around me, binding me exactly as it had in his sorcery chamber. I lay there, useless, my arms fused to my sides, and my legs sewn together. I tried to scrabble backwards, away from the wizard, but I couldn't move.

Filius Canis.

I was furious with myself for allowing it to happen again. The previous trauma of nearly dying in Slyden's enchanted basement smacked me upside the head, and I started to panic. My heart was racing, pushing adrenaline-laced blood to every part of my body. My lungs hurt. I couldn't reach my wand or my crossbow, and I was surrounded by murderous bastards who wanted me butchered. All in all, it hadn't been the best day.

SLYDEN REGARDED me in his cold way, his shining black eyes drinking in my helplessness as I lay squirming against the silk bindings, the hot floor vibrating underneath me.

"You thought I was the black rabbit," he said.

He spoke quietly, and I wasn't sure I had heard correctly, but didn't say so. I didn't think Slyden was a man who liked to repeat himself.

"You thought that Blimaex was the white rabbit, and I was the black rabbit."

I wondered then if Slyden had lost his grip. I wouldn't have been surprised. He was the ideal candidate for Rasping Delusional Syndrome, especially with his foray into the Dark Arts. But I didn't think his mind was diseased: he was too sharp, and too powerful.

Then I clicked. He was talking about that fairytale for wizard children. The one in Abarim Manor that the boys had read when they were children. The words of which he had, seventy years later, magically and cruelly carved into his brother's skin.

"I can't believe you would do that to another wizard," I said. "Never mind your own brother."

"He stopped being my brother when he disowned me," said Slyden. "My family betrayed me."

"You have Abarim blood running in your veins," I said. "No matter how cold it is."

"Silence!" he shouted, banging his staff on the floor and sending red sparks flying, and making Lysander flinch.

Maybe Slyden didn't have Abarim blood anymore. Maybe he had sacrificed it all for his position of power with the Silvanos. Maybe his body was heartless, bloodless, running only on the power he stole from others. I remembered the illustration on the cover of the book: twin rabbits, yin and yang, against a nebulous green and blue fog with gold veins running over it. The title had also been embossed in gold.

THE DREAM DRINKER.

"THAT'S WHAT YOU WERE DOING," I said.

That's why the wizard was so powerful.

Slyden's black eyes burned in my direction.

"Those nightmares Blimaex was having. You were siphoning his power."

The evil wizard in the book was keeping the young girl wizard prisoner in a tower so that he could drink her dreams, or, in other words, take her power from her. That was till the rabbits tricked him to free her, but unfortunately there didn't seem to be any rabbits on the train. Just a furnace that was edging one way, and vampires creeping the other.

"You're worse than them," I said, lifting my chin at the vampires, and they began hissing at us. Their patience had run out, and every single one of them wanted to be the one to sink their dirty fangs into my neck. I must have seemed irresistible, bound up like that in black silk ribbon. A beetle on its back. One vampire in particular was inching closer to me, perhaps hoping to get a head-start on the buffet.

SUDDENLY, there was a deafening explosion in the front of the train. Our coach wobbled on its tracks, almost losing traction and careening off into the blur. The blast knocked Slyden forward, and he lost his balance, falling awkwardly against a seat. I heard something crack: a loud, dry sound, like a bough breaking in the wind. If he felt the pain of the breaking bone, his face didn't show it. I wanted to jump up and take advantage of Slyden's fall, but my arms and legs were trussed up so tightly I was losing sensation in them. Besides, I had other problems. The buffet-crasher's lips were an inch from my nape as I tried to squirm away from him. I could hear his breathing, hot and fast in my ear. A wave of revulsion moved up my body and I closed my eyes momentarily to fight the pictures that flashed in on me. My parents lying, drained and dead, on their bed. The scarred vampire watching me from the corner.

I shouted in frustration and anger. Then I remembered that I wasn't in Slyden's basement anymore, and, unlike last time, I could use my magic to escape from this binding. The fresh grief I felt for my parents was like a tsunami in my chest. Rolling, sparkling, mighty, it rose up, ready to crash and destroy. I shouted again, this time yelling *"Rumpis!"* while I imagined the ribbons tearing. I forced my arms away from my body and jumped up off the rattling floor, the ribbons around my legs shredding as I moved. Slyden looked up at me, shocked. I hurled a fireball at him—*Fiat Fulgar!*—and it hit him in the chest, then disappeared. I hurled another one, more powerful, and again it evaporated as it hit him. There was a slight grimace on his face, so I guessed something was hurting him. I was wrong. He was just gathering his strength for his next spell.

His wet black bottomless eyes never left me. I was about to sling an *Impedio* at him, to freeze him, if only for a moment, but I worried he'd smash it back at me, and I'd be incapacitated again. It was too risky. I pushed my palm in his direction, going after his staff with a *Contendis*. He was too fast for me. Those evil eyes of his locked into mine as if they were slimy black leeches. They pulled at me like black holes, vacuuming me into a limp state that only moved in one direction: toward his deathly white face. He was lulling me into a dream state, mesmerizing me—no doubt a skill picked up from hanging around his vampire pals—and he was drinking my magic.

Usually the fear I felt in situations like this would feed my power, and I'd be able to use it to augment my magic. But now all the grief and panic and anger flowed out of me and into Slyden, making him stronger, still. He sucked up all my emotions, and my will to move, as my muscles lost their tension, and my mind slowly began to follow suit. He hypnotized me into a wakeful slumber. My eyes were still open, but my body was fast asleep. I felt everything leaving my body, as if my whole essence was being absorbed by the dark wizard. I could no longer speak or move my face. All I could do was watch as Slyden drew everything from me, until I had less than nothing left. I collapsed again on the hot vibrating floor of the train as it sped toward the rock face. The last thing I saw was the countdown clock. It showed that we had three minutes until we reached our (final) destination, then everything faded to black.

CHAPTER 38

THE PRODIGAL DINNER

I had fully expected never to wake up again, except maybe in the Afterlife, but when I opened my eyes, Lysander was there, pulling at me, telling me to get up.

What's going on? I wanted to ask, but my mouth wasn't working and I was too empty to say anything, even those three simple words. The fire was creeping closer, and Blondie was urging me away from the heat.

It doesn't matter. I wanted to say. *Burn now, or burn in three minutes, what's the difference?*

My eyes flicked up to the clock. Make that one minute, forty-six seconds. Still numb, I glanced at Slyden, who looked like he was in his own trance: arms shaking, eyes rolling back in his head, like a congregant in an unholy enigmatic church. The vampires knew this was their last chance, and they descended on me. Lysander did his best to fight them off, but they no longer cared for his authority. Pale faces hissed, showing their stained fangs, as they surrounded me, ready for their prodigal dinner. Lysander kept struggling against them, but as soon as he dispatched one vampire, it was replaced by another three. My only consolation was that when the train crashed, it would take the fifty vampires with it, and the world would be a slightly better place.

Then I thought of the voodoo doll in my pocket. If the train crashed, it would also take Blimaex Abarim with it. I couldn't give up. I didn't want to die, and I couldn't let Blimaex die, either.

A RAVEN FLEW above my head, and I thought I was dreaming. It perched on the back of one of the coach seats and looked at me, squawking.

It couldn't be, I thought. *Could it?*

With a loud snap of its wings, the black bird transformed into a young boy with jade buttons for eyes. It was my apprentice, Bron. But something about him was different; the meekness I was used to seeing in his demeanor was gone. In our most recent lesson I had taught him to feel the fear, and use it.

I've been practicing, he had said to me earlier that morning.

Bron had already weighed up the situation while in his avian form, and was ready to act. With a quick jab of his arm he snatched Slyden's staff, which brought the dark wizard back to blinking. The wizard thrust his hand out, ready to destroy the sneakthief, but before he could utter a spell, Bron pointed the staff at him and shouted *"Impedio!"* and the wizard had no time to defend himself. Bron's spell froze him in that pose. The boy whipped around toward the vampires and pointed the staff at them, red sparks flying in warning. They began to retreat.

"BRON!" I managed to say, and looked at the clock. We had sub-thirty seconds to escape the hurtling train. Bron took his eyes off the vampires, and Lysander grabbed his arm and wrenched him up. He yelled and kicked at the vampire, and shouted *"Rumpis!"*

The destruction spell blasted up out of the staff, but instead of hitting Lysander, it barreled toward the ceiling of the train and blew a huge hole in it, letting more air rush in and stoking the fire on board. There was another explosion, and we all ducked and tried to protect our eyes from flying debris. Suffocating smoke swirled around us. The flames leapt everywhere, greedily burning everything in their path. My coat kept the flames away from my skin, but I couldn't breathe, and the heat was overbearing. I was being broiled alive. The stampede of vampires were shouting and screaming, trying to break the safety-glass windows to escape. They stepped on each other and threw punches in their panic to survive.

I stood up, unsteady at first, but the adrenaline helped my body wake up from the trance. Bron shouted in despair as the flames lapped at his legs. He was still struggling against Lysander, who, feet on fire, threw me an urgent glance.

"Ready?" he said.

"Ready," I nodded.

I jumped onto the seat next to me, then hopped up onto the back-rest. I used the silver pole of the vintage glass divider to lever my body up, then kicked off against the wall, parkouring just high enough to reach the hole in the ceiling, which I grabbed with both hands. The metal—newly cut and still smoking, courtesy of Bron's *Rumpis* spell—sliced into my palms as I used it to pull myself up from the burning carriage. With the top half of my body outside the train, I could see the mountain at the end of the tracks. I guessed we had less than twenty seconds before we slammed into it. I hauled the rest of my body up, onto the roof, and the force of the wind almost sent me flying off the top of the train.

"Nano! Helmet!" I shouted, and my collar transformed into a hard helmet and locked around my head. I looked down through the hole and saw Lysander looking up at me from the flames beneath. He tried to launch himself up, but the weight of the boy was keeping him down. I wanted Bron to turn back into a bird and fly out, but I knew the fire was too hot, and would destroy his feathers.

Twelve seconds.

"*Volas!*" I shouted, sticking my arm down through the hole. The rushing wind stole my words, but the spell still worked. Lysander gave Bron a final lift and the boy floated up to me. I grabbed him and pulled him out of the flaming coach, but as he reached the top he no longer needed my help. As soon as he felt the blast of air he snapped into his raven form, and flew up, into the sky.

The huge gray rocky cliff loomed, and the metal I was kneeling on was burning the skin off my knees.

Nine seconds.

I looked down into the coach again, and in the chaos of sparks and smoke I saw Slyden unfreezing from the *Impedio* spell. He had his evil eyes on Lysander, and I assumed he was planning on using him as a ladder.

Lysander bent his knees, about to launch himself up, but Slyden made a grab for him. The vampire made it halfway up toward the hole torn into the ceiling, but Slyden caught the edge of his cape and brought him back down. I looked up at the mountain, struggling with the wind that was pushing me backwards. I had to get off the train.

Six seconds.

"Volas!" I shouted, and reached down to Lysander. It felt as if the fear zipping through my body dashed down toward the vampire. He felt my magic and stretched his hand up, and together we created enough upward force to break Slyden's grip and lift him out of the barreling death trap. Once Lysander was clear of the melting metal of the train roof he grabbed me so hard that I couldn't take a breath. Slyden's clawed hand reached out of the hole and gripped the edge of the glowing steel, his old skin

burning and smoking. He shouted as he tried to lever himself through.

Lysander, still holding me so hard I thought he'd crack a rib, bent his knees, then pushed up off the roof of the train, into the fresh blue sky. We slowly sank down to the wild grass field below, and watched as the *Olde Worlde Railway* steam train hurtled into the mountain with an almighty explosion, sending all hues of sparks and flames blasting into the air.

EPILOGUE
BLACK TIDE

I arrived at my apartment building burnt, bruised, and bleeding, with a serious case of the need-to-get-to-beds. The neighborhood drug dealer—Lou—caught sight of me and her eyes shone from under the shadow of her hood.

She looked me up and down, sizing up my appearance: shredded clothes, singed hair, blackened skin. "Ordinary day, then?"

I stopped walking. "I didn't know you had a sense of humor."

"There's a lot you don't know," she said, quinine iris flaring.

I shrugged. She was probably right. I waved and carried on toward the Swift, a bright spot of red leaking through my bandaged palm.

. . .

I marched through my bedtime routine in a trance. I couldn't feel anything but a dark numbness. I didn't feel happy about saving Blimaex, or standing by while his brother burned. I didn't feel proud of Bron, or grateful to him for overcoming his meekness, confronting his fear, and saving my life. I felt nothing. Whatever Slyden Abarim had taken from me had died along with him in the train crash. I still had that dark vacuum inside my body and nothing would ever fill it up.

Usually, after a day like that, I would have a good cry in the shower while I scrubbed the ordeal off my skin. It would release residual muscle tension and subconsciously help me to process the trauma so that I could leave it behind, to hunker down in my Ghost-laundered pajamas and have a deep, dreamless sleep.

But there were no tears that night, and no emotions. They had been taken from me by The Dream Drinker, and I wasn't sure if I'd ever get them back.

On my way home I'd visited Abarim Manor. I explained to Blimaex and Willard what had happened, and they were extremely grateful, if not shocked. Blimaex was a completely different wizard to the afflicted man I had met after the Belore funeral. He was healed, and healthy, and dressed in a pristine robe. He said he was looking forward to getting back to his work on the Council. I handed over the carved doll in his likeness, and he couldn't stop looking at it, perhaps amazed at how such a small, childlike thing could have caused him so much pain.

Thank you, he said to me, clasping my hands in his. *I owe you my life, and more.*

Willard paid me, and Blimaex gave me the poignant gift of the fairytale book—which I wasn't quite sure I wanted, even with its happy ending—and I slid it into my bookshelf.

The bookcase made me think of Liz Durison's little black book, the EverShade courier's notebook, and Ghost, who had not yet welcomed me home. It also reminded me of the small bottle of *Spiritus Morbus* which was burning a hole on the shelf.

FINALLY CLEAN, with my teeth brushed and pajamas on, I climbed with a deep groan onto my bed. Every muscle ached, and I was so sleep-deprived that my brain may as well have been a cloud of cotton wool. I put my head down on my specter-plumped pillow, looked at the damp-stained ceiling, and exhaled a huge breath that I felt I had been holding all day. I switched off the bedside lamp, closed my eyes, and waited for sleep to wash me away in its black tide.

Then I waited some more. And some more. I tossed and turned, waiting for sleep to come. I hadn't slept in days and my body was more weary than it had ever been. What was the problem? Maybe the fact that Ghost had not yet dislodged the red hardcover book and slammed it on the floor. Was he trying to tell me something? That my day was not yet over? That there was still something to do before I was allowed to rest?

. . .

Or was it because of Lysander? Our connection made me feel intensely uncomfortable. I felt like I had entered into an unholy alliance with one of my greatest enemies. He had saved my life, and I had saved his... and I doubted our relationship would end there.

I rubbed my eyes and sighed, then leaned over and switched the bedside light back on.

I screamed when I saw who was at the foot of my bed and scrambled backwards into the headboard in fright. He was dirty and dripping with blood, and holding something behind his back.

"Filius Canis!" I shouted, once I could talk again.

"Sorry," Darick said. "I didn't mean to frighten you."

"What the hell happened to you?"

"I'm okay," he said. "Superficial wounds." His facial expression was grim. One eye was swollen shut, and his torso was leaking blood. He was full of bruises and lacerations. I scrabbled off the bed and told him to lie down, grabbing towels and a dusty first aid case which contained an empty bottle of antiseptic and a single plaster so old, I doubted it would stick to glue.

Before he lay down, he showed me the shoebox he had been

hiding behind his back. It had holes in the top of it, like a child's silkworm box.

"What is it?" I asked.

He held it out to me, and I lifted the lid cautiously. The creature flew at me, and all I saw was a blur of white fur and whiskers.

Could it be?

"Gizmo!" I shouted, and the ferret pressed its pink nose up against my neck.

"Gizmo!" I said again, and Gizmo leaned his warm body into mine, and then the emotions that had been missing rushed up and knocked me over, and I held onto his small body and I wept into his fur, which smelt bitter and sulphuric, and made me wonder where he had been.

Darick was lying on the bed now, his chest heaving with shallow breaths.

I stood there, wide-eyed, looking at the huge gash on his torso. He was the one with healing powers. What I knew about first aid was dangerous, but I was desperate to help him.

"What do I need to do?"

"Just lie with me," he said.

I climbed onto the bed, gingerly, and embraced his brave body, which twitched in pain as he breathed. His blood soaked into my pajamas.

I couldn't stop the tears. I clutched Gizmo to my aching chest and took turns weeping into Darick's shoulder and Gizmo's fur. I wept for the Belore twins, who were freshly orphaned and on their way to the Copperfield Institute. I wept about the V-Cult victims, all nine of them, and for their families, whose grief must still be raw and overwhelming. I wept because of Lysander and the part of myself I had given up by entering into a relationship with him; a part of myself that I couldn't scrub clean in the shower. I wept because the Silvano Clan now had the HighFire Crown, and things were going to get really ugly in the Realm. I wept because Darick was hurt, and I didn't know how to help him. Mostly, I wept out of gratitude and relief, that Blimaex was healed, Slyden was dead, and Gizmo was home.

After what seemed like hours, the release felt complete, and finally the sobbing stopped.

"Thank you," I whispered. I didn't know what Darick had to do to get Gizmo back, but I'd be grateful to him for as long as I lived.

"Jax," Darick said, and I pushed up on my elbow to look at him. I sniffed, and wiped the last of my tears away. As I looked into his eyes I felt a deep tenderness, an intimacy I'd never felt with anyone before. He gave me that grim expression again. "Jax. I've done something terrible."

In the next room, the red hardcover slammed to the floor.

∾

THE END

ALSO BY JT LAWRENCE

FICTION

WHEN TOMORROW CALLS

• SERIES •

(Futuristic kidnapping thriller)

The Stepford Florist: A Novelette

The Sigma Surrogate

1. Why You Were Taken

2. How We Found You

3. What Have We Done

When Tomorrow Calls Box Set: Books 1 - 3

(complete)

URBAN FANTASY

BLOOD MAGIC

(complete 6-book series)

1. The HighFire Crown

2. The Dream Drinker

3. The Witch Hunter

4. The Ember Isles

5. The Chaos Jar

6. The New Dawn Throne

CURSEBREAKER

(complete 6-book series)

1. The Dusk Reapers

2. The Haunted Portal

3. The EverShade Ring

4. The Obsidian Castle

5. The Pick Pocket's Curse

6. The Eternal Betrayal

STANDALONE NOVELS

The Memory of Water

(steamy psychological thriller)

Grey Magic

(witchy magical realism)

EverDark

(urban fantasy)

SHORT STORY COLLECTIONS

Sticky Fingers

Sticky Fingers 2

Sticky Fingers 3

Sticky Fingers 4

Sticky Fingers 5

Sticky Fingers 6

Sticky Fingers: The Complete Collection:

Books 1 - 6: 72 Short Stories

NON-FICTION

The Underachieving Ovary

(memoir)

The Indie Author Game Plan

www.jt-lawrence.com

www.ingramcontent.com/pod-product-compliance
Lightning Source LLC
Chambersburg PA
CBHW050600190726
48283CB00007B/2221